Little Fortified Stories

Caitlin Press Inc.
3375 Ponderosa Way
Qualicum Beach, BC V9K 2J8
www.caitlinpress.com

Text design by Vici Johnstone
Cover design and artwork by Barbara Black
All images copyright Barbara Black, except the image on page 165, *Woman Smoking*, which is courtesy Alex Mihai from Unsplash.

Printed in Canada

Caitlin Press Inc. acknowledges financial support from the Government of Canada and the Canada Council for the Arts, and the Province of British Columbia through the British Columbia Arts Council and the Book Publisher's Tax Credit.

Library and Archives Canada Cataloguing in Publication

Little fortified stories / by Barbara Black.
Black, Barbara (Barbara Lynne), author.
Canadiana 20240340159 | ISBN 9781773861401 (softcover)
LCGFT: Short stories.
LCC PS8603.L2436 L58 2024 | DDC C813/.6-dc23

Little Fortified Stories

Barbara Black

Caitlin Press

CONTENTS

Origins—9

DISTILLATIONS   11

Port
Old Love—14
Amber-Tinted Tea—15
Lake Creatures—16
Fernando António Nogueira Pessoa—17
Doce—18
We No Longer Have to Whisper—19
Everything Transfixed—20
Blood and Oranges—21
Bruised Mango—23
I Am Real—24
Nocturne—25

Gin
Stitching—28
Like a Lotus Untethered—29
Gotunabe—30
Oblivion Skies—31
Small Tenders—32
Just for the Record—33
The Transformation of Miss Emily Evans—34
The Bones of Amundsen—36

Bourbon
Mount Pedernal at Sunrise—40
Crgizl—41
Barker's Quality Wood Floor Cream—42
Wrong Constellations—43
The Fuel That Stokes My Musings—44
The Map of My Wanderings—46

Tequila
Invisible Ink—50
Tibicina Corsica Corsica—52
Brisk Polka Dancing up Her Spine—54
Old Stories That Are Still True—56
New Moon—57

Scotch
Mothers and Daughters—60
Amapolita Olorosa—64
Little Felt Men—65
The Angels Fall on a Day with No Rain—66
We Do Not Lie Down—68

Rum
What the Mouth Knows—72
Playing With Matches—74
The Hazards of Flight—75
Naukrate, Mistress of the Sea—76
A Thin White Humming—77
Eternal Summer—78

Whiskey
Observations from a Visit to the Museum of Saint
Barbara—82
Salon of Mirrors—84
Feral, Flora and Spore—86
On December 8, 1971, John Albright Dreams He Is a
Snowshoe Hare—87
On the Edges of Where We Live Lurk the Untitled
Masterpieces of Our Dreams—88
A Model Wife—89

THE UNSEEN   91
Lowercase Sisters—92
What May Console Those with the Loss of Their
Lexicon—93
Ink in a Dye Bath—94
The Brothers Cisoires—96
Fishboy—97
Where Women Go in Middle Age—99
My Tiny Life—100
The Tide Rises—102

VISUAL PROVOCATIONS   105
The Path to Inspiration—106
Daughter of the North Wind—107
The Miraclous Ruine of Seinte Romhilde
von Rothenburg—110
Bitter Queens and Foundlings—112
Love's Season—114
Fire Dancing in the Dark—115
Free Divers—117
Where a Dark Heart Burns—119
Because I Am So Often Alone—121
The Town Tale of Dr. Weep—122

ANCESTRAL FABRICATIONS   125
Child Bride, Hawkesbury, Ontario, 1918—126
Granny Larocque, 1892, Russell, Ontario—127
Dark by the Crashing Dark: Francois Xavier
Larocque—128
Last Pinhole to the World—129
The Jaeger Family Theatre—131
Sister Eugénie's Wonderful Glass Eye—133
Herring Radio—134
Fever, N-Gong Hills, Great Aunt Calla, 1953—135

What She Heard as Music—136
Francois Xavier Larocque: Method for the Afterlife—137
Arthur Alexander Finds His Métis Wife, 1897—138
Motiveless under the Orange Eye—139
Each Cell of Your Body a Tiny Clock—140
A Recipe—141

DISORIENTATIONS   143
Knowing How to Find the End—144
Advice While Staying in the Maasai Mara—146
As If the Outline of a Country Had Appeared on My
Face—147
I Know the Plans I Hav 4 You—148
Your Subterranean World—149
Kafka's Dream Diaries—151

FADO 155
Fado I—156
Fado II—157
Fado III—158
Fado IV—159
Fado V—160
Fado VI—161
Fado VII—162
Fado VIII—163
Fado IX—164
Fado X—165

NOTES AND REFERENCES   166

PUBLICATION AND AWARDS   174

ACKNOWLEDGEMENTS   179

ABOUT THE AUTHOR   180

The unnatural and the strange have a perfume of their own.

—Fernando Pessoa

ORIGINS

Deep in a corner of the dimly lit Port Wine House in an
eighteenth-century palace in the Bairro Alto district of Lisbon,
the waiter sets down before me three small glasses with different
samples of Portugal's most famous spirit: port. I settle into
the quiet room, with its wood-beamed ceilings and shelves of
illuminated bottles. My intention is simply to sip, to savour. But
as the wines wet my tongue and their flavours blossom in my
mouth I discover that each small glass contains more than the
origin of a unique taste and aroma. It contains a story. A little
story, its words fortified by voices and images rising as if in a
séance, from a very particular Portuguese spirit.

After Lisbon, stories based on spirits kept materializing.
Gradually, the collection grew to include pieces derived from my
ancestry—liberally interpreted—as well as stories inspired by
music, travel, artwork and dreams.

DISTILLATIONS

Visitation
from Songs of Childhood

Summer night, a girl
sleeps in the milky light
of crescent moon.

In the dark, seasons change
and snow fills the room.
Pygmy owls tap their song.

A presence is there,
neither fire nor air,
observes her eyelessly
till she is altered.

A white moth comes
in the wind, one silvery wing,
brushes her skin
in moonlight.

—Barbara Black

Port

Burmester LBV 2007, Porto Rosso

OLD LOVE

Let me tell you about old love. Half of the sun still glowed on
the horizon. There was a drop of olive oil on her bottom lip.
I loved opera, but his soul was fado. I was arias. He was laments.
Warblers hiding in the oak trees stopped singing. The air swelled
with a cessation of sound. Her voice, which once vibrated the
chandeliers of the Teatro Nacional de São Carlos, now seemed to
come from a very deep well. *When we met, notes fell like dark fruits
from the sky.* She swept her hand and the birds in one motion flew
away. *But I knew in his veins there was a black river. So one day I
said, 'I love you. You are free.'* Now I kiss only the air.

Gran Cruz Tawny 10 anos, Porto Branco

AMBER-TINTED TEA

He hears a faint heartbeat. Above the plane trees. Clutching and releasing. The rhythm of Lisboa. Seated at the Miradouro de São Pedro de Alcântara, he is courting a rose. A rose whose perfume has distinct boundaries and proprieties. He can't just lean in to drink it. He has to approach with an invitation, which he doesn't have. And already he's too late. Sadly, the rose has just passed the peak of her fragrance. He will have to remember how, every morning, she would sit in this garden, sip amber-tinted tea, and place the teacup on a glass table without making it clatter. And how, down below in Avenida da Liberdade, someone was always baking a dish containing cloves.

LAKE CREATURES

The Three Faces of Fear. These were the names their father had given them. Not Sofia, Rosa, Vitalia. The sisters' greatest secret was to have their ears pressed up against the wall of their father's library. They did not swoon over boys (forbidden) or fancy clothes (forbidden). Despite their young age they were elegant, intense. They loved, above all things, books. They craved the touch and smell of inked paper and the words that rose from it, like a strange perfume. But despite their desire to consume all the world's books they were barred from the library. Only men and cigars were permitted and complex considerations on the goodness of God, the benefits of slavery and which Portuguese pastry was better: *fat from heaven* or *a nun's belly*. There was the question of the lake and the part it had played in the girls' disappearance. It was designed to be viewed from the library window and to reflect the sun at an exactly calculated time of the day. At this time, as the father stood looking out the library window, the footman would go down to the dock with the wheelbarrow and dump censored books into the water. Some said the girls had turned into lake creatures and fed on the pages at the bottom.

Vista Alegre 20 anos, Porto Branco

FERNANDO ANTÓNIO NOGUEIRA PESSOA

It's midnight. He's gone to the docks at Rio Tejo, wheeling his wooden trunk. It's heavy and awkward but he enjoys the burden, hefting it past the cranes and warehouses. It contains, perhaps, all that he is, all that he conceals. All that he yearns for and all he's come to despise. He would like to disburden himself of it. Rain patters on the planks of the dock. His silhouette is reflected in the warehouse windows, multiplied in facing panes, each one a different version of himself. His boots don't fit, as if they belonged to someone else. He steps away from the trunk and stoops to adjust them. It reminds him of the white-skinned redhead he once loved. Malvasia. How she would genuflect to tie his shoes, her amber hair falling around her shoulders. How she played only the white keys on the piano. He'd shown her the wrong version of himself. A fiction. *I am no one,* he mutters. His one and only love married an opium-addicted monocle-wearing naval engineer, a man so unlike him and yet similar in some inscrutable ways. Now she spends her life by the sea watching ships pass in the night, loving a man whose shoes fit perfectly. He leans far over the dock railing, contemplating the depths. Below, a multitude of minnows shine in the light of the street lamp. *Is each one identical to the others?* he wonders. His round glasses, like two loose portholes, fall into the waters of the Tejo. He slips over the railing to retrieve them, despite being unable to swim. The old trunk full of unfinished writings sits on the dock. In the light of day, somebody will find it.

Gran Cruz Colheita, 1992, Porto Rosso

DOCE

Feral dogs surround the fruit vendor, their teeth like daggers.
The boys laugh, slip around the back of the shop and grab
armfuls of mangos and oranges, perfectly ripe, tear off the skin,
leaving a trail of peelings all the way to the Piscina Municipal.
She's there again, the thin-legged girl, her long legs brown as
cinnamon sticks. When she walks by, a fragrance lingers in the
air. Something sexish, irrepressibly alluring. *Doce*, like candy.
Sitting by the shallow end of the pool in their torn leather jackets,
a wordless craving pours into them. They stare like animals
tracking prey, waiting to see what she looks like wet. Stern words
are posted stating to shower before swimming in the pool, but
she doesn't shower and nobody says anything. She stands in front
of the sign, only the words "strictly prohibited" visible, pulls an
elastic band from her hair in the most theatrical way and dives
liquidly off the deep end. The rippled pool dazzles like a knife
blade. She emerges from the water and walks toward them with
a smile resplendent as an Algarve tangerine. When she passes she
flicks her long hair, whipping the water across their faces.

Porto Rosso sem nome (no name port)

WE NO LONGER HAVE TO WHISPER

The man with the ruddy face, a regular at Bar O Corvo Noturno, has not come back for his prosthetic leg. It sits there propped up against the bench, an abandoned half-marionette, gathering the cafe odours: cigarette smoke, bacon and mouldy velvet. In his hasty one-legged exit he'd used his crutch, still chanting as he departed, *The fascist is dead! O fascista morreu!* The widowed waitress with her clownish lipstick grimaces every time she passes the forgotten limb. Her long-gone husband lost his life in the '60s at that Salazar prison hellhole, Tarrafal. From the corner of the bar, a drunken patron slurs repeatedly, *The dictator is not dead!* to an audience of none. The moon hangs like the last apple of winter. At home, the man with the ruddy face dreams for the first time in years. He is on a little wooden raft drifting out to sea toward a floating puppet theatre, both feet dangling freely in the cool North Atlantic.

Quinta do Infantado, Porto Branco

EVERYTHING TRANSFIXED

A summer night, in the bedroom with furniture pale as in a dead
girl's dream. She's asleep in the little princess bed, pillow smells
of heather honey. She wakes in another season. Moon spills its
milky light. Snowlight occupies the room. A force by the window
watches, a presence, a wall of molten ice, neither air nor fire. It
observes her, eyelessly, until she is altered in the too-white room.
She never told anyone, but inside she was *congelando*: cold, cold
as the air in Guarda. She had swallowed the pneuma of dread and
attending, whose only purpose was to tend to the ones who will
witness ferocious beauty.

BLOOD AND ORANGES

He shifts the napkin from the table to his lap. Fork lifted with his right, knife lifted in his left. A slight breeze comes through the metal bars of the aviary, disturbs the Padreiro leaves, making them tremble. He wonders, in the soundless air, if the girls had ever really loved him.

He had found and adopted each one of them and nursed them back to health. *You want to punish me*, his wife had said, grumpily plucking a quail. Unlike her husband, she did not consider them her "children." Algueda, Fernanda, Inez, Paolina, Jenista, Lygia... Here he hesitates. For the last one was the flower of his heart and had a voice so sweet he swears the trees would lean in to listen.

They were spoiled. Rose water sprayed daily in their "boudoir," a place as noble as a silver carriage with a princess inside. A rich diet, fresh air and music-making at will.

What every man of this predilection knows deep in a compartment of his heart is that he is not really a devotee of beauty and music but a jailer.

Before the heat waves when the girls were still here, he'd had a recurring dream that a woman incarcerated for insurrection had escaped through a tiny hole in her cell only big enough for a bird or a mouse. His wife had a dream that she had become a painter and favoured the colours orange and red.

Somehow the new days of relentless scorching stripped away his vivacity. His wife spent her time inside, sharpening her cooking knives and emptying the larder of things past their prime. Every day he yearned for rain. Sweet and fragrant as *Citrinos do Algarve*. He made shades for the girls so they would not overheat. They sang less than they used to. He escaped for hours, taking cool walks by the river.

He will never forget that morning in August. Feathers of all colours strewn about the aviary. At the bottom of the cage lay the girls, ravaged and lifeless. Who could have done such a thing? Rain brought the smell of blood and oranges.

He puts down his fork. Striped shadows from the cage bars cross his face. What a mystery it is to fly free, he thinks. That trembling of air around your wings.

Venâncio Costa Lima, Moscatel Reserva

BRUISED MANGO

She refused to eat the mango bruised by someone's large thumbprint. *Jacinto, peel me an orange like this, in one... continuous... strand.* There was always a competitiveness in her passion, as if any minute she might spit out the fire. He watched a golden bee land on her thigh but said nothing.

Favaios Moscatel do Douro

I AM REAL

Your small garnet eye scans the room for imperfections. You don't realize that your lens is tinted. You see only cherry-lipped angels with luminescent skin, hearts lit up like lanterns, only things that fly and float. To you, I am dull, solid, held down by gravity. Flawed. But when I leave, I'll make footprints in the brick-red earth, ride a chestnut horse, walk the hills of São Brás de Alportel. You will have only the evening light to feed on, and even that is fading.

Geraldino Moscatel

NOCTURNE

There are bits of code in a lament that can ripen a fig. Even a green one. Chopin knew this and embedded these codes in his nocturnes. His cats try to scratch them out of the furniture, especially those in C# minor, which cats find particularly painful. Every piano knows that Chopin wept inside his arpeggios. Treble strings have a direct route to the troubled heart. At this hour, the composer, lacking inspiration, has left the parlor and is taking his rest behind closed drapes. Although instructed never to do so, the maid spies through the gap to make sure he isn't dead. She waits. She watches. His chest is as still as an ironed sheet. But then it comes. From his mouth. Strange shapes. Black dots with tails flowing out of his throat. She's seen them before. Illness? Some are hollow with no tail, like the loop of a noose, which frightens her. They seem to hum. They move toward the curtain as if to escape the room. She's afraid of allowing them access to the parlor and closes the curtain abruptly, but it's too late. In the parlor the piano strings are vibrating like a beehive in a heat wave.

Maybe everywhere he goes with his tattered cowboy suit

and commanding green eye people ask the same questions.

"This is Graciela. Well, *was*." I admired his fetish and suspected

the rest of it was at one time his only friend.

I invited him to stand in the shade of the saguaro.

He looked up at the looming plant with its arms

like a beckoning desert goddess.

"No. I am Gotunabe. Thank you, Mam. I am my own shade."

—Barbara Black

Published in *Cincinnati Review*, Oct. 16, 2019 miCRo (excerpt)

Gin

STITCHING

After piercing the linen with the needle, she falls into narcoleptic
sleep—sews herself into another dimension, spiderlike,
undetected. One, two seconds go by. On another continent, a
lighthouse keeper in brown stockings stacks sandbags in a storm.
Seawater seeps under her door. The sleeping woman smells it.
Three, four seconds go by, although these are different, more
enduring seconds than the usual ones. They pass like butterflies
in slow motion. The woman's mind is a gossamer net, gathering
time. Five seconds. In a high mountain meadow in Norway, a
widow looks out to the peaks beyond, missing her husband. The
sleeping woman's chest contracts. The air is thin. Six seconds.
Seven. A young mother in a tropical country watches her five-
year-old hang from a guava branch. It's too high. The child
doesn't know. Eight seconds. The sleeping woman's eyes snap
open. A boy skateboards past her window. It sounds like a train:
ka-lak, ka-lak, ka-lak, ka-lak. She pulls out her last stitch and
starts again. For the body has its own time and the stitch can be
revoked.

LIKE A LOTUS UNTETHERED

The pool was the sky, filling with thunderheads. The colour he'd wanted for the water was azure, but it was later in summer and now the clouds had turned it an ominous grey and green. This would be his last day of mourning for her.

He covered the water's surface with slices of lemon, each one topped with a fuchsia flower, to remind him of her eyes. On the patio table he placed a bleached horse's skull with a rose. Death and beauty were a natural pairing. In the west, clouds kept amassing like tumors.

His final drink sat in the holder of his floating chair. He would drift in the pool among her eyes like a lotus untethered, until the sun expired and the palm fronds quivered like a dying bird. Until snakes crawled out of the hot plaster walls to escape the heat even they could not endure.

GOTUNABE

The boy lumbered to the gate, body swaying back and forth. I gave him the warm glass of water he had asked for. The lid on his one large central eye descended. *It tastes of tears.* His pant cuffs were frayed and an odour of overripe cucumber came off his body. *I don't have no home,* he answered, when I asked where he lived. I wondered how the world was for him with that large monocular view. *Freight trains come from far, far away. But when they pass it's like they'll drive right through my middle.* He seemed to have perceived my thought. Or maybe everywhere he goes with his tattered cowboy suit and his commanding green eye people ask the same questions. He pulled a chicken foot from his pocket. *This is Graciela. Well, it was.* I admired his fetish and suspected the rest of it was at one time his only friend. I invited him to stand in the shade of the saguaro. He looked up at the looming plant, its five outstretched arms like a beckoning desert goddess. *No. I am Gotunabe. Thank you, Mam. I am my own shade.*

Ungava Canadian Premium Gin, Ungava Spirits Co.

OBLIVION SKIES

A heron stood sentry at the front door, handing out beaks. I
didn't like mine. It was a crossbill's beak, a pine cone-picker's
beak, short, with the tips crossed over, which made me look
goofy. It required a special adaptive straw. I felt it hindered any
opportunities to meet other more exotic birds. It caused me to
lisp. What a strange place. Party lights made from pendulous
Montezuma oropendola nests woven from banana fibres. Bird
bath finger bowls. We couldn't choose our own cocktails, despite
there being more enticing names on the drink menu such as
"South Seas Elixir" and "Oblivion Skies." We had to wait in line
with our name and a number engraved on a rare Great Auk egg.
My assigned drink was an overripe avocado green and tasted of
macerated oak leaves and mustard. Not even a hint of pine! A
clump of swallow-beaked guests huddled by the buffet, talking in
their passerine way, some gathering clumps of spinach dip and
hummus as if readying to make a nest. When I spoke to them
they didn't understand my warbly dialect, but laughed drunkenly
at everything I said. I could never tell if I was uproariously funny
or unintentionally comical and inept. The raptors had descended
from their overlook on the mezzanine to raid the buffet. A
chilling hush overtook the party. A large woman with a status-
flaunting velveteen cape wedged in beside me, shredding canapés
with her vicious hooked beak. She turned. I saw my future in her
bark-brown eyes. *I'm not here for the finger food*, she said.

SMALL TENDERS

I've been trying to hide from my life my whole life. I had a kiss
once on my lips that burned. I let it linger there. I never wiped
it off. It was as if my insides had unfolded slender yellow petals
I never knew existed. Then the winter came. And never left.
Every morning I poured a bucketful of water over my head in
expectation of a visitor. I did this for thirty years until one day
the visitor appeared, in the still of winter, when everything
was concentrated into tincture, one scent prominent: witch
hazel. The visitor appeared at the gate. Tall, over seven feet, she
approached me, shuffling through the crust of snow. Breath
visible, as if a soul were escaping her body. Her hair was ribbons
of cedar cones. Their essence of *thuja* reached me before she did.
She greeted me by shaking her mass of dry cones and extending
a basket full of what looked like small tenders of meat. Although
they didn't move, they looked somehow alive. She gestured to
choose one, to put it in my mouth but never to swallow it. I
followed her instructions, its dense texture strange, warm, inside
my mouth. I felt... a fullness. Words began knocking at my rib
cage to escape. Snow shrank away from my feet. She placed in
my palm a red berry. It had a singular power like a planet in
its creation. Was it poisonous? She gave no instruction about
consuming it. As I held it there, the season changed. And she was
pleased. Her arms retracted into her body. Her lips moved, but I
heard no words. I saw that she did not have a tongue. When she
turned to leave, her back was the trunk of a yellow cedar.

JUST FOR THE RECORD

Was it an accident that a black word became a crow and a white word a dove? And, really, was it necessary to grant "rule over the birds in the air"? They already had their own governance. Crow, in case you didn't realize, knew the word for "sacrificial" long before the gods were invented and even dropped sounds on rock to see what words would burst out. Later, there were whole voluptuous sentences that oozed out of an oyster shell and, with luck, a pearl as an end stop. Crow came up with articles long before that other God pointed and named. "The" was quartz grains or red ants. Prepositions? Shrew eyes and thistle seeds. Yes, if you want the truth, look to the avian sector. Ay-ee-ii-o-u? Songbirds. Doves, for example, invented the vowel sound "oo," which has been in use ever since. Of course, being doves, they never bragged about this. Crows and doves have had a bit of a battle trying to get their vowels and consonants to work together. And just for the record, diphthongs were invented by the Great moaning Potoo to terrorize humans in the night. Finally, heron with its long, particular and exacting beak, was elected to assign punctuation, done only in solitude of course, when no one was looking on and disagreeing. So, sure, Creator by his own account "dashed off a bird," if you want to believe that. But next time, call on the birds and they'll give you the real story.

THE TRANSFORMATION OF MISS EMILY EVANS

The report by Dr. Blanchford Corrigan claims that Miss Evans's obsessive study of Spinoza had induced a mania for unorthodox freedoms that were not becoming of an unwed or even of a wedded woman. As her intellect burgeoned beyond the boundaries of polite society, and explosive notions of feminine agency split her corsets causing her dress hems to curl up above the knee, the hideousness of her heresy became all too obvious.

Dr. Corrigan immediately confiscated her Spinoza. And her microscope. She was prescribed oil of oregano (to purge atheistic urges); hot sage baths (to sweat out delusions of the relativity of evil); and thrice daily enemas (to evacuate mind- and body-infesting philosophic tendencies). All this did little more than clear her bowels. They screwed her thumbs to the table, trepanned her skull and subjected her to repeated readings of Samuel Forçon's breviary of morality cures. Still, her intellect expanded.

A conjuror was summoned—actually, the conjuror's old wife in disguise: the conjuror had died ten years previous and she'd assumed his identity. She built a ring of fire around Miss Evans, uttered a curse in a language that sounded like the clatter of splintered whalebone on tiles, and tossed at Miss Evans's feet "dead canaries" (corn husks wrapped in napkins). Miss Evans disappeared in a veil of smoke. When the smoke lifted, there stood a low shrub with oblong leaves, vivid golden flowers and berries which proved to have healing properties.

The Ethics Council, uninterested in botany and unschooled in the Ovidian transformative arts, declared the curse a success. In secret, local women called the plant St. Sophia's Wort and made a concentrated alcohol from it which they shared in their reading circles and found to be an especially good accompaniment to Mary Wollstonecraft and cigars.

THE BONES OF AMUNDSEN

Six degrees above the horizon. That time of dusk astronomers call "the golden hour." An albino spider, as tall as a house, strides across icy tundra, a man between her pedipalps. You don't see *her*. You see the flickering shadows of her legs elongated by the sun's low angle.

She used to be called "Maman." People don't believe she exists. They took her children, her beautiful spiderlings, to study—"rare albino anomalies." Up here, no one will look for her. Even if they did, no one would see her against the stark white of the arctic snow.

The man wriggles in her grip like a wingless insect. One of her eight eyes might have seen you, frozen there on the knoll. But stationary objects don't interest her. She craves the moving, the living. For a time, anyway.

Back in her nest in the abandoned research station, she builds sculptures and wind chimes from the bones of Amundsen and others who come and scratch in their diaries, trying to understand things that don't need to be understood. When the wind blows through the storm-blasted windows, the chimes play a brittle symphony of human death that makes the hairs on her eight legs stand on end. The sound reminds her of a delicate walk on the strands of her web, the crystalline feeling a mother knows that at any moment things could go wrong, leaving you to squint into a blinding light.

The beautiful is always bizarre.
—Charles Baudelaire

—Barbara Black

Bourbon

Booker's True Barrel Bourbon, Small Batch, Kentucky Straight Bourbon Whiskey, 6–8 years

MOUNT PEDERNAL AT SUNRISE

For a year now, Georgia had suffered from intermittent catatonia. It always kicked in when she looked at Mount Pedernal at sunrise. Ralph, with his turkey jowls and age-spotted face, leaned on his ash wood shovel and said, *Old woman brain. Seen it in my mother, seen it in my aunts, see it in my wife.*

It was the Godlessness of the mesa that struck down all words and gestures. Its mean geometry you couldn't argue against. Or praise. It put to bed all those notions about God's hand in the frilly interior of a peony. Each morning backlit by the sun, Pedernal needed neither woman nor man to validate its existence. It was monumental, untouchable. But she thought this only later. Standing before it with her paintbrush in hand, she was frozen by its geological brutality. It stilled her body. There was no paint colour for that.

CRGIZL

It wasn't his choice to have the tongue transplant. He'd made his peace with his own stupidity and his crazed trigger finger. The docs just wanted a subject to practise on. They wanted accolades. But the new tongue mangled his words. When he wanted to say "luckily" the tongue pulled in, humped at the back of his throat and slurred "crgizl." At Ruben's Tackle and Gun shop he tried to thank the pretty cashier but couldn't master that initial voiceless dental fricative. Instead, the tongue flapped to the roof of his mouth and made a sound like a tiny hammer hitting a nail and then a kitten meowing. *Thnk thnk yyyw.* Plan B was speech therapy with a blueblood doc. You could say it was successful, except for one thing: now he spoke like a high falutin' patrician and couldn't stand the sound of his own voice. He moved away from the city. Lived in a trailer in a birch grove where leggy elk strode through like giants from a pagan past. The haughty wolf that daily defecated on his back doorstep agreed to the trade. Now the man speaks wolf—if he even speaks—and the wolf sits at the Friday night poker table, regaling men with his tales of stalking wild horses and luring them into domesticity.

BARKER'S QUALITY WOOD FLOOR CREAM

Varnish. Top-of-the-line varnish. Master craftsman varnish. Mahogany pianos and cherry wood cabinets varnish. Then the smell of tobacco. Fine tobacco: Louisiana St. James Parish perique tobacco. Drifting in from the parlor every Sunday evening at exactly ten minutes past seven. Following the trail of smoke, she knew he sat in the Farrington wingback chair. He never spoke, of course. But his presence made the hairs on her arms tingle. The room felt electric when he was there. After three visits she started calling him Vernon and set a slice of pecan pie on the side table before he arrived. She loved his calm, his presence, the way his fork floated in a gentlemanly way. When he departed, there was always an indent in the chair seat which lasted a few minutes, then disappeared, just like him. The back door would squeak like a cranky possum, then shut. Rumours haunted the neighbourhood. There was a gentleman caller, but no evidence—except the widow chattering behind drawn curtains every Sabbath. Actually, she wasn't a widow. She was what in polite circles we call a "spinster." Other than some girlhood dalliances, love had passed her by. Until now. Despite his lack of corporeality, Violet never loved any man more than Vernon. For the remaining thirteen years, she got on her knees every Sunday at six and cleaned the parlor's maple wood floors with Barker's Quality Wood Floor Cream, then sat down and ate a slice of pecan pie, waiting for Vernon to appear. Tonight she'd passed away in her chair at 6:59. Still, at seven, the hairs on her arms rose ever so slightly.

Russell's Reserve, Kentucky Straight Bourbon Whiskey, 10 years

WRONG CONSTELLATIONS

If I were inside out, I could see it—in the middle, my body's
membranous empty space, an inland sea bereft of its waters. My
womb never stretched. I was an untested levee, never breached
my parameters. Did you know that foetal eyes form from black
dots and later forget what they've seen underwater? The ears are
small submerged trumpets searching for voices from the other
world. Light comes in subtly through skin. Blurred shapes move
past. There is a time, too, when there are no fingerprints and
anything that might be called knowledge is as amorphous as a
just-born jellyfish. What I know now is that I know nothing.
For me, moons came and went, mostly red, then none. I'd been
standing under the wrong constellations. Do you pity me? Don't.
I pulled worlds from my mouth. I birthed new stars from my
pores. I called them Rose-Petal, Peeling Birch, Cloudface and
Agate. I wrote their names on my skin and never forgot them.

Maker's Mark Kentucky Straight Bourbon Whisky

THE FUEL THAT STOKES MY MUSINGS

When JP Sartre pollarded his ash tree into terrified stumps, an arborist came to his door, indignant. *You're butchering that tree! A hack job like this will be the death of it!*

All things benefit from an occasional knockdown, JP retorted, and went back to puffing on his pipe.

There are knockdowns, but then there are *knockdowns.* His phone rang. A voice like a shovel scraping a sidewalk demanded, *You need to stop smoking that pipe! You're screwing up my schedule.* It was the Grim Reaper.

What? You don't even do house calls anymore?

The Reaper laughed and said he was too booked up to get to all his clients, half of whom were never home anymore. *Hardly anyone does door-to-door these days. I had you scheduled for a year from now and here you are sucking tobacco fumes like it's already doomsday!*

That's precious coming from you, said JP, adding, *I'd invite you over, but it'd be the death of me.*

I've heard that line billions of times but—good delivery.

Wait, Sartre said. *What do you mean "a year from now"? Isn't that kind of early? Get rid of my pipe, the one object that makes my existence worthwhile? Even my dog comes second. My pipe is the fuel that stokes my musings. Its plumes frame the hours of my days.*

I can put numbers on those days.

They spoke for another hour on the phone. JP reclined on the couch, puffing away, watching his beloved plumes float up to the ceiling. En-soi, his dog, curled up in his lap as the two callers discussed immortality (Grim Reaper against), euthanasia (Grim Reaper against), and free will (Grim Reaper against).

My grim friend, I find it pretty ironic that you of all "people" have an opinion on free will, given that you rob people of it every day. No one had ever called the Reaper "friend" before. There was a pause.

Listen, said the Reaper, lowering his voice. *Can I call you every so often to chat? We could make a trade. The dog for another ten years.*

THE MAP OF MY WANDERINGS

There was a difficulty with conceiving. I lacked faith, said the
doctor. I hadn't visualized sufficiently "the heroic spermatozoa's
journey" to conquer the female anatomy. I hadn't surrendered my
body to an act of nature. Alright, I said. I went home and ate an
entire pumpkin, coachmen and all. I swallowed a wolf just to see
what it felt like. I danced in a red smock, ate clouds for breakfast
and drank from the rain barrel. I made three wishes on a massive
genie fish I found at the beach. When my wishes weren't granted, I
fried it and ate it for dinner. Meanwhile, my husband sequestered
himself in our unheated garage, head inserted into the innards
of his 1993 Ford Probe. His "baby." In fall, I left to swim upstream
with the spawning salmon. In winter I moved into a mama
badger's den where we gorged ourselves on eggs of darkling beetle.
Mama was good at "I Spy" on those long, dark days, and until then
I never knew there were so many shades of brown. In spring I
hunted musky weasels and dreamed of exponential rabbits. Smells
were the map of my wanderings. I befriended a barred owl. We
almost fell out of the tree laughing, yelling *who-cooks-for-you?* as
the old stars above sputtered like a faulty fountain.

I had faith now in nature's rhythms. I was vernal, diurnal,
nocturnal. Predatorial. My hair grew into wild grass. My eyes
glowed in the dark. The weather forewarned me through the
pores of my skin. I parsed the soil, the rain, the weeds that
lined the riverbanks. My womb was a hive, alive with internal
processes. When the doctor read the ultrasound he looked
alarmed. *Well, I'll be darned. You've got a whole litter in there!* I
looked back at him with my authentic feral smile, careful to hide
my incisors.

You were once wild here. Don't let them tame you.
—Isadora Duncan

Tequila

1800 Tequila Reserva Reposado

INVISIBLE INK

Askar closes his dental practice early this morning. Everyone these days who has money—that is, almost no one—wants blinding white teeth. Everyone without money pulls their own teeth. After removing his crucifix pendant, he closes the office door and, placard secured to the handlebars, rides his battered bicycle to the square. He's been planning this day for months.

11 a.m. He installs himself next to the resplendent fountain anchored by the oversized statue of their permanent president, whose golden tooth glitters blindingly in the sun at exactly noon every day. The air is hot and dry like a summer that's gone on too long. Askar lifts up his placard to be seen by passers-by. His sign is blank. No words to alert the censors. Ironic but not offensive. He used to relish the giddy satisfaction of outwitting their scrutiny. But today he feels no thrill.

12:30. The president's tooth no longer glows. A sudden breeze picks up the edges of the placard. It puckers and wavers in his hand like a wayward sail. He struggles to keep it from getting torn or blown away. He has a brief vision of himself taking flight. Irony may be more dangerous than he'd thought. More dangerous than defying a curfew, his favourite act of defiance in the vanishing past. He smoothes the wrinkles developing on his thin white shirt.

After an hour, Askar has the creeping sensation of an invisible force field from his body repelling the masses—no one has been paying any attention to his sign. He tries to look insouciant. His brain seems to be casting silent words and exclamation marks out into the square: *Freedom of religion!! Government for the people, not the censors!!!*

At 1:17 a police officer approaches and grins at his fresh victim, his mouth full of rotten teeth. Askar suddenly feels as if he's holding up a giant white lollipop. The officer's distended belly (the envy of every citizen) juts out, as if a shark had swallowed a whale.

Eh, you can't protest.

I'm not. It says nothing.

But you're protesting something.

It doesn't say anything!

But you're thinking it.

The officer circles around Askar, sucking air through his teeth. He does it a second time in reverse, right hand fondling his firearm.

Does that bike have a licence?

Yeesss, Askar stumbles. He explains that he forgot it at the office. The beer belly expands like a hot air balloon as the officer draws a deep breath. Out of habit, Askar reaches for his crucifix. Thankfully, it's not there.

The officer grasps Askar's arm firmly. *You can't protest against nothing.* With his other hand he reaches for the handcuffs.

Espolòn, Tequila Blanco, 100% Puro Agave

TIBICINA CORSICA CORSICA

Today he'd seen the hummingbird hawk-moth, *Macroglossum stellatarum*, believed to be extinct since 2024. Another victory. And a fine example of convergent evolution. His daughter Lise logged it in the notebook after they'd taken lunch on the veranda—whenever that was. He'd stopped winding the clocks. There were so many insects now in their plantation he could tell time by their behaviours and calls. There was no need for clocks, barometers, thermometers or even a compass. Nature transmitted all the information they needed.

He'd corrected Lise when she'd said "Our Eden." She was young. She thought everything was a beginning. There were moments when his love for her cohabited with a deep love for humanity, a fear of its extermination. In his mind it made her change from his daughter to something utilitarian—although altruistically so— which he couldn't abide, conjuring up crash survivors consuming the dead. His reading today was about subversion and sublimation in Baroque garden culture. He was not convinced that ornate fountains had anything to do with repression by the state. The book was mouldy, which he disliked, and he was interrupted at the juncture of the second and third chapters by the rising pitch of *Tibicina corsica corsica* in the heat of the day, a rising beyond the sonic at which point *Homo sapiens* declares there is no song, where the cicadas talk only amongst themselves, male to female, or only amongst the equally highly tuned. The screeching made it impossible to think. In fact, these days, insect song and thrall had become so intense he hardly felt like thinking or speaking at all. As if he and Lise had become insects themselves.

Lise reached up to pin his shirt on the line. Through her cotton shift, the sun showed the curve of her waist. This was the hour when the nectar rose in the lantana. The hummingbird hawk-moths would soon appear, fluttering like linen in the wind.

BRISK POLKA DANCING UP HER SPINE

Hildegarde, plush with fur, was a bon vivant and never flinched at her follicular abundance.

She'll never marry! Never! laughed the young men in the bar when Hildegarde's name came up. Secretly, they were all in love with her. The greater their love, the larger their bombast. Exuberant toasts chipped beer steins. Backs were slapped too hard. Erections hid under hats.

Hildegarde was not just born, said her mother, she demanded to be born. Eleven hirsute pounds pushing and kicking to get out. And her cry—the highest note of a Puccini aria, breaching the walls of the house: *I'm alive!*

By age six the girl had a convincing moustache. By ten, a beard. She began riding horses and learning the accordion. At age fifteen she grew the most beautiful furred breasts. When Hildegarde turned seventeen, her mother invited suitors on Sunday afternoons at four. Many men wanted to court her. But no men came. Instead, they spent the day in vigorous activities dampening their ardour. All other girls seemed to them now like pale sticks with ghostly voices and skin like the wrapping on sausages.

Time passed. Hildegarde didn't fret about her lack of suitors. She learned how to lasso a calf and practised Puccini and polkas on the accordion. Her parents were proud of her. Every evening her mother brushed her daughter's abundant hair while *Chi il bel sogno di Doretta* spun round on the record player.

At age nineteen Hildegarde took up beekeeping. This was how it happened. Honeycombs were running with honey. The huckleberries were gone and the bears were hungry. Normally, this was the time everyone brought the rifles out and propped them at the ready by their back doors. Hildegarde didn't believe in firearms. What nature provided was a gift to everyone. She had just sung her honeybees to sleep *sotto voce* and stayed out in the evening to feel the cool wind in her fur.

He was large. The largest she'd ever seen, a coat with an auburn sheen. But despite his size he looked thin. He stood up on his hind legs. She felt excitement—a brisk polka dancing up her spine, a high note, a shimmer. He sniffed the air, reading its scents. Could he smell her, she wondered? In her beekeeper headgear she might even look like a bear. He didn't approach, got back down on all fours and headed straight for five hives, ripped four apart in a frenzy, dipping his tongue into the honey, pure joy on his face. Bees accumulated on his chin, a crawling, living beard. He licked his paws rapturously like a preening cat, did a waggly dance and made a chuckle-growl that tickled her deepest parts. He left the fifth honeycomb for her.

When darkness fell and stars filled the sky like a million luminous bees, young men lay in bed and felt the sting of a love they were too timid to pursue.

On the table, a note from Hildegarde to her parents not to worry, she had found her true love.

Gran Centenario Tequila Añejo

OLD STORIES THAT ARE STILL TRUE

I once met a man with only one tooth who called himself "Añejo" and who pointed at the sun and said, *We are all born sun, but burn up with our unrealized possibilities. That is the real cause of death.* I gave him a five-dollar bill, went home and decided to learn the cello. Things happen out of order and only make sense in hindsight. I did not learn the cello as it turns out. I go to the jungle where the leaves sweat and odours of minuscule dose hover in the canopy. Silhouettes dance in the filtered light. Here, your teeth ache with possibility. Your eyes become jaguar. Jungle smells, more nuanced, more layered. Your alphabet changes to the glyph of a three-toed bird. This is how you find a lover who until you arrived was one of the unloved. The visual hunt is an illusion, my friends. Our insistence on this is laughable, regrettable. The eye is the least poetic organ. *Let me wear your skin* is how the other senses speak. This is the beginning of how we find each other. Two light beams meet in the undergrowth. The round back of a gold beetle like a shining eye looks down from a tree upon this unfolding. When the two lovers collide in the tangled thicket, the beetle chews through a *wanuxlua* flower, showering them with a sticky residue that assures they will be linked together forever.

NEW MOON

It will happen in the meadow. It will happen when the elk calls out for a mate. But it will happen only if the moon is a sliver in the night. If he comes with his heavy coat and his heart in his hand. It will not happen if the moon is full. It will happen if I'm full of the love I have for him.

Look. Look in the sky. Tonight there is no moon at all.

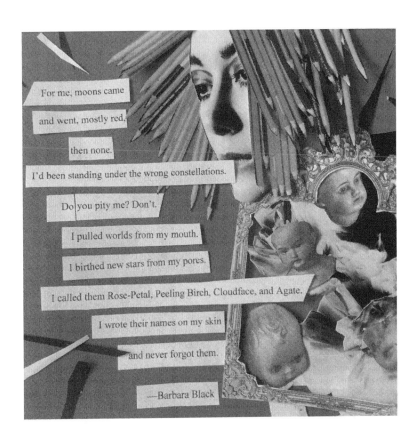

For me, moons came

and went, mostly red,

then none.

I'd been standing under the wrong constellations.

Do you pity me? Don't.

I pulled worlds from my mouth.

I birthed new stars from my pores.

I called them Rose-Petal, Peeling Birch, Cloudface, and Agate.

I wrote their names on my skin

and never forgot them.

—Barbara Black

Scotch

MOTHERS AND DAUGHTERS

I

I walked into a landscape of dry hills. Up a very long ladder, which extended into the sky, was a woman with her head inside a cloud. She was waving a net made of kerchiefs and old underpants.

What are you doing? There's nothing up there to see, I called up.

Exactly what my daughter would say, she answered. *I'm catching moths for their powdery dust. Up here it's night. Once this net is full, I'll scatter the dust over her bed while she sleeps, to seal dreams into the bedclothes. Without dreams, we're just sleeping animals.*

Are they good dreams?

That's up to the moths.

II

She startled me, the woman with sprouts in her chin and hair rolled up in tin-can rollers. Dressed in coveralls, she was laying out a dirt plot with traps constructed of broken tools and appliances. Rows of sharp metal teeth and mashed gears glinted in the sun.

Don't bother me! she barked, as I opened my mouth to speak. I watched her roaming up and down the rows as if inspecting ranks of soldiers. *She'll step into every one of these, that daughter.*

But why? I asked, horrified.

Because I set them. I know her.

III

There was a clothesline. A woman with breasts as enormous
as bread loaves was hanging up babies by their diapers. Babies
chubby and wrinkly, thin and wizened, late born and too-early
born, pinkish and bluish, brown-eyed, hazel-eyed and green-eyed
bobbed up and down in their diaper slings each time she pushed
the clothesline out.

Hello! I called, coming up the path of wildflowers. *That's a lovely
collection you have there!*

Thank you, she answered with a voice as warm as milk.

Are they all yours?

*Oh, no. They're not mine. These are all the babies my daughter could
have in her lifetime but never will.*

Never? How do you know that?

*Because I'm a mother. Still, I'll take care of them all, these little
possibilities.* She plucked one from the basket, pegged it up in its
diaper and whisked it down the line.

IV

Striding in the distance, a woman dressed in a cape threaded with
dangling bones. I picked up my pace to catch her.

Who are you? she asked.

Oh, nobody.

Are you somebody's daughter? She eyed me sideways.

Yes.

Then you are somebody, she said. A gust of wind threw her hair up vertically. Her cape alternately filled with air then deflated as if her clothing were breathing.

Why are you wearing those? I pointed at her cape.

These are the bones of daughters who died before their mothers. As I walk, their voices are heard through the clashing of bone, heard by mothers alone.

I told her that it seemed a poetic type of remembrance.

Sometimes. Some mothers hear it as music, others feel the voices in their own bones as the most excruciating cellular pain. But still, they want to hear it.

V

A stunning lake high in the mountains. Clear and depthless. A bowl of blue. On the slope my mother stood, tossing small stones one at a time into the water.

Mom, I greeted her. Oddly, we did not embrace. This was not a reunion.

What are you doing here?

I'm throwing rocks.

You never did that before.

It's just what is done here, she replied. *Each stone is a secret a mother was not able to tell her daughter.*

Have you thrown in yours?

Yes, just now.

We stood overlooking the lake, the fathomless blue of her eyes averted from me.

The rings travelled concentrically ever wider, ever weaker, like a spoken word fading into inaudibility.

Oban Little Bay Single Malt Whisky

AMAPOLITA OLOROSA

The father walks alone behind the second, smaller coffin, a
tiny gown nestled in the palm of his right hand. Behind him,
someone sings *Amapolita olorosa de las lomas de Guerrero—Little
fragrant poppy from the hills of Guerrero...* This was the daughter
he had prayed for when the crops were plentiful and his wife's
hips still swayed to the sound of the *guitarra*. Long ago, his right
ring finger had been crushed in a plow. The ring, too. When his
brother saw the finger, he said it looked like the crooked stick of
a shaman. *Hermano. Bad luck follows you like a masterless hound*,
he'd laughed. After the funeral, the patrón's wife offers the
father a child's music box. It has a spinning ballerina with a pink
porcelain skirt, but the tune is broken. Still, he takes it and winds
it every evening again and again, until the sun goes down behind
the Sierra Madre del Sur, drowning in a pool of orange.

Arran Single Malt 2016, Traditional Oak & Oloroso Sherry Cask Finish

LITTLE FELT MEN

Friedrich Schiller could write only if there was a rotting apple in his desk drawer. Simone de Beauvoir had little felt men sewn into compartments in her undergarments so that she could crush them when sitting. One of these is untrue, yet compelling. I've been following the leafcutter bee as it handily snips circles from fireweed leaves. These are the scrolls it carries under its belly when it flies like an enchanted Talmudic scholar to its secret library of expectant pupas.

Johnnie Walker Red Label Blended Scotch Whisky

THE ANGELS FALL ON A DAY WITH NO RAIN

At night the sleepers appear, naked, in intimate poses, floating across the town's crumbling walls. When the sun withdraws, we gather on porches and smoke. With shaky hands we lift our cracked cups to our mouths and drink what averna we have left, its taste bitter-sweet, like life. We watch the sleepers pass: the large-hipped woman fused with her smaller husband who twines around her lovingly. The "falling angels," spiraling around each other in a never-ending dream. There's a struggling, tumbling man who shields himself from danger, a posture we understand. From what past do they come, we wonder, as they drift by as if in an unseen liquid.

We watch the sleepers instead of eating. Instead of making love. Instead of sleeping. We envy their weightless world. We sense we're becoming weightless, too. When Father Sanfilippo left us for the new town, his robe dragging through the dirt like a tattered prayer, we reclaimed the church. It was broken, just as we were. Now we survive on sorrel soup, blanched chicory or the roots of mountain asphodel. A lack of expectations has freed us. Each morning we worship at the cracked church bell of Chiesa del Purgatorio, nestled in the rubble at the top of the hill. Our hands tremble in prayer. The ground shifts slowly beneath our feet.

Tonight there are tremors at dusk. It doesn't stop us from watching the sleepers. Across the north wall, a youth with crescent moons carved into his chest glides by on his back, contemplating the stars. There are no lights anymore in our town, only the light from the night sky. We pass around the averna until the last drop is gone. Across the old walls, an emaciated man is dancing. Perhaps there is still always something to celebrate. The last sleeper is Lone Ophelia clasping her breast, swept along by the streams of time, still searching for an end to her story.

Glenfiddich Single Malt Scotch Whisky, 12 Years

WE DO NOT LIE DOWN

On one of the three lakes the ice was imperceptibly breaking up. Her red coat was a pool of blood against the snow. Goshawks strident in the pines screeched like hard-bowed violins. Rage and rebellion. This was always his way. She smelled diesel from the rail yard. The lingering winter made you feel as if a piece of you had died.

If the ice had not been perilous, if the children outside had not screeched *We'll kill all your horses!*, if she'd cooked the rabbit as he'd demanded, it would have been different. But the tenderness of its limp paws. The wisp of red at its throat. He called it "the gift of winter" when animals lost their camouflage and stood out against the snow. He especially liked hunting rabbits. In his previous life he'd been one, he said. By eliminating them he believed he could preempt the cycle of reincarnation and the possibility of becoming one again. Ideas like this sprouted from his brain like hyper-fertilized seeds.

The rabbit's brown fur, smooth as velvet, spoke of winter branches. To have stripped it off and parcelled the animal's beauty into pieces was more than she could bear. He fumed at her hesitation and went with his set mouth and ear-flapped fur hat to ice-fish instead. Animals were the lower ranks.

No matter where they lived in the city her grown son, like a stray dog, always found a wild patch somewhere. Sometimes he hopped the regional train to find them. Scrappy lots sprouting gorse and rusty car parts, hidden forests forsaken by people, haunted by coyotes, or a swimming hole swarmed by carnivorous plants. It was his way of staying alive. But it was an illusion that he blended into these places. What he sought was to assert his spot at the top of the food chain. He ate whereof he wilded. He lived a camouflage life.

At the third lake the birds sounded more frantic. The leader of the search team spotted the boot prints. She tried to convince herself they did not look crazed. Hauled up onto the ice, her son was, finally, still. She felt in the marrow of her bones the terrible beauty of him. He looked like a child again, bewildered and open. It would only be later that she would discover that the lakes he called Cody, Crocket and Carson, after three famous hunters, were not known by these names locally. He had branded his personal geography.

In the passing days, melting ice dripped off pine boughs, leaving pinpricks in the snow. The slow drip in her heart began. She remembered believing as a child that bird songs were notes floating on the winter air. How do they sleep at night with no nest to protect them? *We sleep standing up*, she heard them answer. *We do not lie down unless we are dead.*

A heron butler handed me my beak. I didn't like it: a pine cone-picker's beak, short, with crossed tips. It made me lisp.

It was a strange party: lights made from Montezuma Oropendol nests. Bird bath finger bowls. We were each assigned a number engraved on a Great Auk egg.

A large woman with a velveteen cape was shredding canapés with her vicious hooked beak. "I'm not here for the finger food," she said, sizing me up. When she darted toward me, I fled down the fire escape, tossing my beak into the basket of a Schwinn bicycle.

~Barbara Black

Rum

Goslings Black Seal Bermuda Dark Rum

WHAT THE MOUTH KNOWS

Last night I sent a telegram to my mouth which wasn't speaking
to me. It read *mother, mother, who gave me my mouth, I have no
voice without your love.*

> There are times in your life when it feels as
> if the sun has reached down with a knife and
> cut you into small fires.

When I was fourteen I gave a bath to my mouth because it was
dirty. It screamed at the sight of soap. It said *to be clean frightens
me more than death. Cut off my lips, but don't make me clean!*

> When I was six, my mother washed my
> mouth with soap because I said *Damn!* After
> that strange man removed my clothes, I died a
> little. I could not speak. I should have shouted
> *Damn! Damn! Damn!*

I made a mask without eyes, nose or ears. When I formed the lips,
they said *daughter, where is your voice? I have already lost your face.*

There are different kinds of mouths: cupid
bow; full lipped; thin lipped; straight; or the
downturned mouth that occurs before a death
like my mother's.

In Rome, St. Teresa's mouth was open in ecstasy as if rapture and
pain had converged.

You need your mouth in the afterlife to speak.
The words coming from your mouth won't be
heard as they are in earthly life. Instead, like
moth wings tapping skin, they will be *felt*.

The Kraken Black Spiced Rum

PLAYING WITH MATCHES

I recall little watery vials with flecks of gold kept in the fancy cutlery drawer. Yes, you can drink the memory of something and hold it inside. It burns like a small flame the way hope can be contained in a thimble. Children in the past loved to play with matches when toys were scarce. Flames had a way of accelerating childhood, just as fairy tales were a crude medicine for confronting reality. Red Riding Hood would have preferred a purple wool coat with metal buttons, not a cape. It could have made all the difference. She might have met a Princely Wolf in a satin doublet and silk hose, not a backwoods cross-dresser with a taste for old ladies. There is always that feeling in life that we are about to be undone.

Two Drifters Signature Rum

THE HAZARDS OF FLIGHT

Your paper wings crackled in the air as if the skin of a snake
moult had taken flight. Where was your sense of geography in
all this? On land you thought everything was flat. But up here
the sheer fecundity of shapes and undulations invigorated
the imagination. Mountain ranges like a beggar's spine.
Knolls rounded as a mossy breast. Far below, now fading, the
inconsequential shapes of the earthbound. In your chest a
sensation quaked and quivered. You did not know you were
what the sky craved, not the other way around. Were you the
offspring of a demiurge who wanted sky to test the viability of
humans? No, it was a trick. The sky allowed your suspension for
a few moments. But then your wings faltered, even as you were
thrilling with the weightless substance of you. As you fell, you
saw yourself reflected in a lake below, a slim shadow plummeting
into sky—but a sky whose surface could be broken. You survived
as far as your cunning and craft could carry you. You, with
your candle wax dreams and wood-frame wings. But the land
reasserted its laws.

Wax? Every housewife and kitchen slave knows that wax breaks when it's flexed. And it's not an adhesive. I was there in Crete, in the court of Minos. Of course, nobody mentions that, what with *labyrinth this* and *Minotaur that* and a woman having it on with a bull.

It was I who caught the swans and painstakingly plucked them for my husband's elaborate collegiate dinners where the conceited and insufferable bull-man held court with his crude animal jokes and sour breath. I had gathered and cleaned the feathers, as requested, unaware of my husband's plan. But I did not make that pathetic flying contraption.

After Daedalus killed our son I plotted my own escape. After all, who best knows how to make an escape? An aging engineer or a former slave? All women, being chattels, have a natural understanding of flight. No one would suspect lowly me, Mistress of the Sea.

I concluded that the solution lay not in imitations of birds but in imitations of sails. No wax and feathers required. Just scrap wood from my husband's crazy maze and a large linen sail cloth. I fashioned my own "flying" apparatus and calculated the winds that would land me in a different life far from Crete.

You think I can't know winds? Simple observations. The spiteful winds, the mothering winds, winds that bring the locusts. There are the bone-chilling ones that whisper your fate. And breezes that once carried my loving words to my son.

A THIN WHITE HUMMING

We curled together those long nights in satin sleep, listening
to each other's music, notes landing upon us like pollen grains.
We were the original silent violin. Nobody else could hear our
songs. We were "shadows," they said, but they were the ones who
couldn't see in the dark. They didn't know the possibilities. You
in your Gothic long coat, me in my organza batwing dress, our
nectared tongues licked stars from the ceiling and then, kisses
soft as guava flesh. All lives have a frequency and ours was high.
While those in the dark were dead asleep we were sipping from
moonflowers, evening primrose and phlox. Until you disappeared
one day in the light.

I flew over rooftops to track your scent. My searches for you
were echoless. Near the cathedral belfry a code hit my chest. A
thin white humming. I followed its call. I made an image of the
destination. I arrived with my Braille-ears on alert. You were
there in the grass, brittle in sunlight. Wide-eyed. Glass eyes.
There was no breath.

I brushed the pollen from your face. Seven men stood nearby
dressed in large-sleeved robes. When they saw me they knew that
for you, my love, the sleeping soul, the journey was done. Already,
you were flying back into the velvet black of your origins.

Nothing is something else. Love is neither like an ember nor a
flame, nor an echo or a void. But if I must answer, I'd say it's like
a bat cave, dark and sequestered where, for a lifetime, we hang
upside down and see with our ears, our heartbeats lost amongst
the heartbeats of a hundred others.

ETERNAL SUMMER

The doorknob was a hand, elegant with elongated fingers, like his mother's. Sandor grasped it gently as if in familiar and tender greeting. The door swung open. Beyond, was a trader's market in a vast hall of booming echoes where vendors hawked wares of all kinds. But all were faulty or broken: ruined 20 gauge shotguns, tools with dulled edges or rusty blades, battered duck decoys like the kind his father obsessively carved, vintage hunting gloves with holes in the fingertips or pairs of only lefts or rights. He approached a stall where a woman with deep green eyes and chunky hands hunched over a collection of shoddy knick-knacks. *How much?* he asked, picking up a snow globe with no snow inside it. *Ah, that,* she reached across and grabbed it from him, *I call 'The Eternal Summer.' Watch.* She shook the globe vigorously and set it on the table. The water bubbled and foamed, then settled. Sandor saw himself as a boy, in his bright orange jacket, playing alone at the lake's edge where his father had left him. On the far shore, ducks bobbed in the water. Above, clouds hung like latent dreams. He loved the mallards, the males with their iridescent green heads and cream-coloured bodies that made them stand out on the water, the females whose dun camouflage protected their young. But he was mad at them for being duped, for not knowing they were surrounded by wooden imposters complicit in their deaths. *The lake in Ujvari Woods! Oh, I've lost my little rescue boat...* Sandor leaned closer to look into the scene. Deep in the thickets, barely visible, his father stalking through the underbrush with a shotgun, in search of targets. *...that was the day someone shot me in the arm!* Sandor cried, reaching for the globe with his good hand, but the green-eyed vendor snatched it and threw it to the ground, scolding, *People see all sorts of nonsense in these things.* The water slowly leaked out. Sandor felt ill. He knelt down, weeping like a child over the broken globe. *It's not for sale,* the vendor said. Sandor remembered his father's carving knife going round and round, peeling the orange flesh of the wood block, willing it into life like Collodi's Geppetto, except that each time the block would yield a mallard, not a son.

Medusa moaned for a thousand years that there was no god of unruly hair.

Her snakes would rattle like glass ropes in the desert. "What if I created

my own demi-god?" Her hairdresser disapproved. There was already a god. The general one.

"God's a kind of hole," she said, unconvincingly,

and combed the snakes with a rubber rake.

When Medusa returned home

from the salon of no mirrors, 400 years and as many snake
skins had come and gone.

"Why must I suffer a centuries-long bad hair day?"

Medusa coaxed the snakes off her head

with rodent hearts and honey.

It was that easy.

She had never considered their freedom. Only her own misery.

The lightness of her scalp felt like sky settling on skin.

—Barbara Black

Whiskey

OBSERVATIONS FROM A VISIT TO THE MUSEUM OF SAINT BARBARA

1. St. Barbara of Nicomedia, my holy namesake, offers protection from lightning, kitchen explosions and mid-life detonations.

2. We regret that the saint's head and left hand are missing.

3. Only when Saint Barbara was headless did she gain authority. In what way does this make sense?

4. Confined in her tower, she painted blood-splashed canvases with just one hand. Fire in its many manifestations. The first small, quivering flame. Voracious bonfires. Conflagrations of the heart that consumed entire landscapes. The saint herself, however, is said to be fire-retardant.

5. Alternate legends say Saint Barbara carried her head in a goat skin purse and applied lipstick to her pallid lips. This is apocryphal.

6. Once you are a martyr you are no longer a woman.

7. No one ever dared call her "Barb" for the flesh-tearing implications.

8. With St. Barb by your side, the storm will have passed and the lightning vanished before you could say *Dad's your killer.*

9. The saint's right hand is kept in the Monastery of Saint Michael in Kyiv. The glove covering the hand is changed frequently. Pieces are given to pilgrims. It is so quiet in the crypt you can hear the heartbeat of the guard who stands vigil, his fixed eyes like two steady coals.

10. Many admiring electricians, miners, explosive experts and laymen who do not understand fireworks drop by the saint's tower to squeeze prayers into the building's crevices. The paper flutters in the wind like captive birds' wings.

11. The saint's tower has three windows: one to see god; the next to look down on Van Eyck's masons toiling to finish the never-finished tower; and the third window to cast her glance toward the hard edge of the world.

SALON OF MIRRORS

Why is there no god for unruly hair? Medusa moaned.

Her hairdresser insisted there was already a god: Zeus. The general one. *God is a kind of hole*, she said, *you can pour your heart into*, and combed the snakes with a rubber rake. Medusa huffed, *I can tell you what kind of hole*, and the snakes did a harem dance atop her head.

The only difference between your hair and mine is yours is alive, said her ornitrix, addressing the less dangerous back of Medusa's head.

... and it's self-braiding! Medusa quipped. *Take that, fancy Miss Aphrodite.*

The salon was mirrored from top to bottom. Everywhere ornatrices or clients looked they saw Medusa in duplicate or triplicate, but never face to face. To never be bestowed a glance was a worse fate than ugliness.

Above, Zeus tracked Medusa's conversation. Zeus had a scissor mind: half open, half closed, snipping through the flimsy fates of mortals on any whim brought in by the winds. Zeus was impulsive. Medusa was not. On a daily basis she had to plan her every move.

Years passed. Many snake skins came and went. Time charged on like a crazed centurion bent on victory when victory was no longer possible.

It was a desiccating summer night. The snakes, growing old with their host, slept coiled in a serpentine chignon atop Medusa's head. Along the walls of her bedroom, the stone figures of her many former loves kept vigil, faces frozen in terror.

Why must I suffer a decades-long bad hair day? Medusa lamented. The desert wind exhaled its hot breath through her window. It often spoke to her in this way. A hissing whisper, not unlike snake-talk.

One rat heart, one egg. One rat heart, one egg. A line from her bedroom out the front door. She lay down on the cool tile. Waited. The snakes slithered from her head like the severed tongues of those who have defied the gods. It was that easy. She had never considered their freedom. Only her own misery. She understood now how hair was vanity. The lightness of her scalp was sky settling on skin.

She closed her eyes. She was going down to the sea again, on the isle of Sarpedon, where waves moved back and forth, languidly, like desire.

FERAL, FLORA AND SPORE

Three languages. *Feral* is his choice for communication. A marital clash always causes a sloughing. He sheds his skin to show an argument of arteries and muscles. The muscle is the premise, the arteries the explication. If the argument is refuted, he has to reclothe in his skin and find a quarter moon at which to howl. Then begin again. It's exhausting always proving oneself, proving one's wild side, the slip and sway into the slime. On rare occasions he resorts to *Spore* to talk of larger issues. She never does. *Spore* talk is a dark brown, textured mathematical code which, when dispersed, activates the solar system, where the conversation takes place. It can accommodate vast philosophical quandaries. But it often takes millennia for anything to be understood. His wife spoke *Flora*—especially *Swamp Lily dialect*— which is why it never works out for them. *Swamp Lily* put them at odds with each other, setting their teeth on edge with its damp vowels and murky observations. When she felt secretive or threatened she spoke *Prairie Grass dialect*, a susurrating slide around s's and an urgency that always seemed to him below the threshold of his hearing. This may have been intentional. His wife was adept at molecular communication, knew ways to subvert him with covert machinations in the subsoil, reprogramming his cells, lowering his defenses. No, he would remain above ground, faithful to *Feral* and peel off bits of himself to leave along the path as clues.

Jack Daniel's Tennessee Sour Mash Whiskey

ON DECEMBER 8, 1971, JOHN ALBRIGHT DREAMS HE IS A SNOWSHOE HARE

I never seen one. But I was one. All white 'n' fluffed and big feet. I'm driving my pickup in a blizzard. This fox, never seen one, runs across the road. My wife, because she's a chicken, squawks like hell on wheels at which point I realize my back paws don't reach the pedals. Wife turns up the radio, blasting out *I am woman hear me roar.* One long slo-mo skid ends in a roadside fox hide and a slide-slam into the flank of Finn's Peak. Right. Inside. The mountain. It's pitch black and through the windshield all's I can see is a jumble of roots and granite. Truck is dead. I look at my wife. She's changed into some kind of shaman with this fancy chicken feather head dress, fox-fur and army boots. Reaches for the door handle, turns to me with these gleaming eyes and says, *This is where I get out, hon.*

ON THE EDGES OF WHERE WE LIVE LURK THE UNTITLED MASTERPIECES OF OUR DREAMS

There is a fever, they say, that turns your thoughts into flowers. Is this what I have? I thought, shedding pink roses. I walk the streets and people think I'm a wedding, sidewalk awash with violets. O voice of dreams and the door to implausibility! Have I married myself?

A MODEL WIFE

After her career as a model in Saks Fifth Avenue, fashionable, long-legged Amy—well, most of her—was carried away, horizontally, by a man with short arms and a serious face who erected her (perhaps that's the wrong word) in his living room, seated in the brocade princess chair in his former mother's summer dress. Her chair was quite hard, whereas his was padded. Although Amy's facial expression was somewhat static, if pleasant, her hands were very expressive, despite missing a few fingers. During sessions of night-long lectures while he marched back and forth across the carpet orating, she remained, without fidgeting, as if in deep reflection, never interrupting his refutation of Nietzsche's theory of eternal return.

NECESSARY aNGEL tHEATRE

a nobody's dying—
brittle in dusk,

Witness

white humming...

sweat. Moonlit-white-Alone-milk,

Everything frozen melody,

we dream

the moon is A

GHOST SUN

we light every lantern

—Barbara Black

THE UNSEEN

LOWERCASE SISTERS

God's eye is closed. We float on a moonless night, haunted by the image of the nuns sewing penance cushions. Scant starlight staggers through willow branches like strands of wayward sin. Life, now, is liquid. We've forgotten how to pray. Small beads of memory bring back our childhood songs. Bella sings them quietly as we slide through the channel. Pitch always eluded me except when climbing up pines. But Bella was born with a concert hall in her chest—a fortissimo all-enveloping voice. Father buried it in an old nail box in the garden. Our legs are cold from kneeling in the canoe. No altar, and still we genuflect. But such language of the body can change. This darkness we move through we do not suffer. Now we are lowercase sisters, as we were in our butterfly days. We know where the nail box is. We already dream of flicker-lighted rooms where our real names are embroidered on swan's-down pillows.

WHAT MAY CONSOLE THOSE WITH THE LOSS OF THEIR LEXICON

A woman stands against a brick wall and sings my songs all day.
How does she know me? She, with her crooked brown teeth
and voice like a rusty pair of scissors. She has a sack at her feet
which, they say, contains: a piece of fabric from the glove of St.
Barbara's right hand; a pocket watch stopped at 10:45; and a tiny
vial of frankincense. Every day, a boy passes by and asks for the
same song, which she sings while he dances in his ragged clothes
like a crazed marionette on fire. The air in that square smells of
melted beeswax. As soothing as an old memory with none of its
details, only its lingering sweetness. The wagoner passes by with
his squeaking cart full of mouse fur slippers which make me want
to cry. The woman sings my words. The merchants stop their
hawking to listen. And yet, I have no words anymore. They've
abandoned me. I'm no better than the ratty curs, hanging around
for scraps. One day I ask the singer how she knows my songs.
I don't, really, she answers. *When you pass by, your songs follow
behind and I hear them. They're lonely. They float into my mouth
and down to my belly where they ask to be sung.*

INK IN A DYE BATH

Everything between four walls—colourless. Not that I knew what that meant. White dolls with white frocks, white hair, white eyes. Days ashen grey. The lonely black of night. In that hut, Father taught me the theory of colour. Primary, secondary, tertiary. Light waves. Wavelengths. Rose, lavender, tangerine, puce, each name an unknown island. The idea of colour invaded my dreams, bearing strange gifts I couldn't unwrap. What was teal? Like a clap from a bell? Red sounded like a hammer hitting my head. Cinnabar might be a luminous fish on the bottom of the sea. People think if they have a word for something they know it.

One evening as the sun was setting, a blade of colour shone through a crack, casting a strange film on the white tile floor. It seemed to glow. It made my heart pound in my chest. I told Father. He filled the crack. Days, weeks and months went by. I ate meals blindfolded. I studied religiously. My legs grew longer. Father promised me, that for my courage and persistence, I'd be featured in the top scientific journals.

Only when I reached fifteen and Father was convinced I knew everything about colour did he release me. Immediately colour ruined me. It disordered my nerves, it made my body shudder. There were colours that nauseated, colours that screamed, colours that wept like a funeral cortege. I didn't care which was tangerine and which was turquoise, it was a world of excess and confusion and left no space for my eyes or my thoughts to rest. I had my eyes restored to monochrome. Father arranged it. Restored, I wandered the rain-slanted streets, weeping at the beauty of a clothesline, folds catching the low light of late afternoon. I wrote my runaway sister: *At sunset, shadows spread like creeping ink in a dye bath.* She sent me a paint set labelled *Colours of the Rainbow.* She never did understand me or anyone else for that matter. (That's why Father chose *me* for the experiment.) Everywhere I went now, patterns engrossed me: stripes and diagonals. Lines on old faces. A light beam caused raptures. When people remarked on the colours of a sunset I answered, *Yes, the high luminance of the citadel is striking!*

I felt alone. I met a man, but when he brought me red roses I felt none of their ardour. I'd never seen his lips as carmine, but I had kissed them with passion. Wasn't that enough? He proposed to me with an emerald ring. *The colour of your eyes,* he said, his eyes signalling *forever.* I thought it was a diamond. A month later, he left, like a high-wire walker traversing an ever-thinning line. There were others over the years: Alistair, the sensualist, who could not help describing to me the *steel blue of the sea* or the *electric green of a wheatgrass meadow,* as if I couldn't see at all. He was never interested in how *I* saw the world. And Steve, the black and white photographer—a visionary I thought, except that he cheated by shooting in colour and converting to monochrome. I should never have trusted him.

Finally, I asked myself where can I find undying devotion?

I went to the kennels to choose a companion, the blackest or whitest or greyest they had. I surveyed each pen, each lone inhabitant. *That dog with the sad eyes,* I said. The clerk looked down his glasses and answered, *a dog is a mate, a soul you dodged in your first life. He'll love you to death.* I said, *I'll take him.*

THE BROTHERS CISOIRES

They are conjoined twins but not friends, their monocled heads facing away from each other as if in perpetual peevishness. The left leg moves right and the right leg moves left. Is it cooperation or working at cross-purposes? Midriff, a one-button, low-cut vest, shiny as a newborn's head. They only wear the best. They dress sharp on every occasion. If they could, they'd walk upright, silver-striding down Main Street—think of a stiffer Fred Astaire—and through the plaza, slender legs brushing past each other, tapered feet like a high diver's piercing the surface. They have a surgical flair, but dislike being called "a pair." They are precise, but can also be cutting and nasty. One always threatens to leave the other, but without the other they are nothing.

FISHBOY

All day Sunday he sits in the puddle. The sun does set but
the moon doesn't rise. Everyone calls him Fishboy. No one
remembers why. All he's able to stutter is *Not, not, God is not.* To
the children it sounds like *God is snot* and it makes them laugh.
Their mothers slap at them as if slapping at flies. Clouds move
above his head and across the brown water. Actually, he is not a
boy anymore, but no one wants to admit this. A dog's bark cuts
a hole in the air. Through the crowd comes the sheriff and his
mastiff. The boy flaps his arms like a baby duck. The townsfolk
scowl at his big-boy hands—dirty, dirty—as he squooges them
into the mud like a Creator making humans.

Years ago when his sister was here, Sunday nights were always the
hot bath in the zinc bucket on the front porch. She'd move the
washcloth over her brother's skin and he would laugh, slapping
his palms on the water's surface. He loved to play in the dirt,
even long past the time most children stop doing so. *Aslllippee...*
he'd chatter to her in his language, which only she understood.
It sometimes included real words and sometimes not. After, she
would wrap him up in the big towel, singing to him about God's
children and then point out the north star, saying, "Remember, if
you can see the north star you know where you are."

The sheriff moves close to Fishboy. Keys rattle in his pocket. The
boy remembers that sound from the past, late at night above his
room. The crowd inches forward. *Get him up, get him up.* In the
distance a train wails over the river, warning people off the tracks.

What you don't know is the moon has fallen from the sky. They
all blame Fishboy. He was always looking up. First it was the corn

wilting, then torrential rain, now this. Too much strangeness in a single week.

The moment the sheriff reaches for the boy, his dog leaps to Fishboy's side. It sits down in the puddle. It snarls at anyone who dares approach. They all know the viciousness of its bite.

At dusk, the crowd leaves, their plans for revenge thwarted. Fishboy gets up and drips his way home, back to his roofless house, the dog trotting along. He wraps himself in a ragged towel as best he can and lies on the bed, face shining up at the north star.

WHERE WOMEN GO IN MIDDLE AGE

I will be ringed/ At ankle, am a corvid thing.
—from "And Wylde for to Hold," Lucie Brock-Broido, *The Master Letters*

This is my bed: sticks and old man's beard. What I dared to do as want was wild, what I willed was wanton quelled. Here in our raven nest we drink salt water with no harm. Light enters in the gaps—husha, husha—we are still alive. Whether your heart is here is immaterial. I left you in the salt flats licking your wounds, where the undercurrent drowns the weaker fish and fisted tufts of eel grass cut when grasped. Come some time. Come up into the peculiar air. There's a red moon some nights when we sing open-mouthed. Don't recoil. It has its womanly cure. If fog draws in we face north to take a compass point, south if the sea is calm or east for a silver dawn. What is it like? Like a debt paid with fever and then, waking with wet brow, wind breathes on your face. And sometimes a whale passes by.

MY TINY LIFE

"SURVIVAL IN THE WILDERNESS"

Now, the past is a mystery to me, the way a bird can't tell a
window from a mirror. My limbs are twigs, my head the size of
an elderberry. I follow his words and build a survival shelter.
There's mud to cover my eyes for the difficult days and a carpet of
memory to cradle my sleep.

"BURNABY PARK IS CHOCK FULL OF STRANGE TREES AND BERRIES"

Like a dung beetle in the desert dawn, each morning I roll one
huckleberry or blueberry to my shelter. I bite into mushrooms
that are as tall as I am. My maxim: just enough. At night the old
cedars whisper like mothers deep down in the soil. I prefer this
language. There are too many words that aren't needed anymore.
I bury them under rotting logs.

"I KNOW WHERE THERE IS SOME CLAY OF BROWN COLOUR NOT UNLIKE OCHRE"

The clay is soft and brown, as he said. It makes a small bowl from
which I eat. It's like childhood but not the same. Childhood was
always the smell of golden apples, a happiness you could eat.

I live in this small book full of maps and instructions my father left behind. After all the clocks stopped. This is the only way. My cone bract shoes take me to that other canyon, the place of my childhood, where it smells of needled loam and cottonwood sap and time is strands of sunlight splintering through trees. I sit in the licorice scent of bracken. Water echoes through the canyon walls, a liquid lullaby. It's more than survival. Here, inside a hollowed stump, I pass my tiny life.

THE TIDE RISES

The oystercatchers are on the rocky islet, with their comical red beaks and bright pink feet. How easily they live half in and out of water. I can't remember how high the future sea will rise. I'm trying to see numbers, charts, percentages, illustrations, diagrams, measuring sticks. The large oystercatcher waddles to the edge, stabs a mussel like a mariner pinpointing a map. Not an oyster as you might expect. It smashes the shell open, tears out strands of flesh. Riptide is starting in the channel further back. What's the channel called? I forget. It blocks forward movement in one direction but accelerates it dangerously in the other. The beaks look like children's building sticks you'd dump in a jumbled pile then extract one without causing collapse. The oystercatchers make squeaky, tub-toy cries. A small comedy in a salt-water world. Soon, the high tide will drown the islet. You won't, from a distance, even know it's there.

We have art so that we shall not die of reality.
—Friedrich Nietzsche

Crow dropped sounds on rock to see what words would burst out.

Whole voluptuous sentences oozed from oyster shells.

Sometimes a pearl as an end-stop.

Ay-ee-ii-o-u? Songbirds.

Doves invented the vowel "oo,"

which has been in use ever since.

And diphthongs were invented

by the Great moaning Potoo

to terrorize humans in the night.

——Barbara Black

VISUAL PROVOCATIONS

Artwork: *Conscious Mind of the Artist (Subconscious Decision and Actions in Progress),* **Nicole Eisenman, 2007**

THE PATH TO INSPIRATION

See the road? It's always uphill. Orby and The Girl Who Looks Downcast (TGWLD) are on their way to anywhere. Orby, dragging the hand cart, has turned a turmeric colour from the sun. His nose is as burnt as a marshmallow in a firepit. He has the hardest job: having to look ahead. Beside him, The Girl Who Looks Downcast never takes off her red blanket comprised of the tinted dust balls of many a crappy art studio. She never looks further than a foot ahead. To make "extra" money TGWLD, also called Tigwild, knits these dust balls into sweaters for those who love to sweat in the summer—those who put burdens on themselves hoping to flush out the muse. Orby and Tigwild are so busy on the road chasing ideas they had to outsource their work to Reginald, the talented chimp who sits atop their travelling hill of dust poised at the canvas, painting anything that comes into his simian mind. The good thing about Reginald is he never overthinks. They're training themselves to do this but have not yet succeeded. Their greatest fear is that they will reach the end when it's not really the end, just a road to nowhere. Actually, nowhere is where they are most of the time until something gets accomplished, creating a temporary somewhere that makes them giddy for a few days until once again the cart must be dragged up another hill.

Artwork: *Cloud,* Kim Dingle, 1999

DAUGHTER OF THE NORTH WIND

Was she alien or divine? They took her to Reverend Skutch. He drew a hasty cross on his chest. *Bathe her in milk and holy water daily and keep her away from all winds.* They balked at his fears. With her difference, their daughter caused unease yet exuded only love. Their little portent, their divine jester, a laugh like high-stacked cumulus. What all along they'd been missing.

Bunnykins came to them in a blizzard. Frothy and white with black patent shoes, frilled socks and a back full of fluffed blue feathers. Blown in backwards with the north wind, arms outstretched to the polar regions from where she came. She landed in four feet of snow on the front lawn. They gathered her up in a shawl and carried her to the fireplace to warm up. *No!* she shouted. *No fire!* They took off the shawl and moved her away to the armchair. *Mamapapa I'm melting,* she cried, while drops poured into her patent shoes.

In spring they built her a refrigerated playhouse. That red hair of hers was the only hot thing in there. A stream of playmates came and went and, tired of blowing on their fingers to stay warm, they disappeared like icicles in a slow melt, until there were none. One day, boys came shouting and throwing torches. The playhouse was reduced to coals.

Spring gave way to summer. All things wilted and melted. Neighbourhood kids ran screeching in and out of sprinklers. Lawns browned under a scorching sun. Their girl stood in front of the window under the air conditioner, terrified of stepping outside. Once they caught her running her fingers through the gas burner flame. She asked if fire was the way to find friends.

After that too-hot summer, they moved to the north. Bunnykins thrived in that climate, blue eyes sharp and cool as corundum, exploring every undulation of the cool land, shouting, *Mamapapa, look!* Not a lonely child, or an only child, but an every child, casting her attention on every facet of her world: finding bluebirds in the grasslands, wading barefoot in the creek, searching mystery in the woods beyond the fields. Perhaps they let her roam too far from home.

When it was too cold outside, Bunny put on her shiny black shoes and danced for hours in the basement. Tappity-tap: the sound of happiness. Her parents kept up with news from the outside world, hiding their growing alarm at the state of things. Flash floods, droughts, blizzards, heat waves, hurricanes. They still felt safe in their far northern homestead and Bunny flourished. But sometimes she stood for hours at the large paned window, staring. One evening at the dinner table she asked, *Mamapapa, is this my real home?* They looked wide-eyed at each other across the table and said "Of course, of course!" then sat in perplexed silence.

In July, a hot breath rose up from the earth. A sound like infinity forced through a tunnel: hundreds of acres of forest burning their way toward the homestead. The north wind tore across the parched boreal devouring trees, blackening the air. They saw Bunny at the end of the field and called her home. She stood transfixed as the towering smoke column advanced. They rushed out the door, heading down the hill, screaming for her to return. Why was she running toward the fire?

Their red-haired girl vanished in a wall of flames. They found one blackened patent shoe.

Sun rays angle through the window. They treasure the days when fluffy clouds billow on the horizon and the snow glows an eerie blue at dusk. Every Saturday night they put on their clickety-clackety black patent shoes and crazy dance together until the sun goes down and the house grows endearingly cold.

Artwork: *Scivias, Vision XI: Vision of the Last Days,*
Hildegard von Bingen, 1100s

THE MIRACLOUS RUINE OF SEINTE ROMHILDE VON ROTHENBURG

Gryffix, my Soule, my desiringe, my fool and foil.

To be a living Seinte is Hell. Denied every Human emotion, you must feed on Saunctite alone. It is a dreadful and solitarye lyf. I had a thirst for Mortel lyf, and dirt and stryfe and everi passioun. And so did I drink one day wilfulli from the brackish spring in the wood. I was courting Chaunce. No sooner I swallowed that terrybl brew than a strong wrathnesse boiled up in me. It came ferst in the form of a mangey cur who barked and howled through my resistance. I became as foam-mouthed as he. I tether'd hym by the tongue to the Wrathnesse Tree, where he speketh no more. This was the beginning of my miraclous Ruine. A geld that threw me on a ride was nexst to join the Tree. Then a blak ber, a panther and a lioun. My Holynesse fell like scales from a dragon. Soon I had no control of my Mortel madnesse. Until I met dere Gryffix.

Do you knowe the sorowe of looking monstrous, yet being blithe of spirit? Of suffering a terrybl othernesse? Gryffix, the innosent terror of every touneship and dorf from Avignon to Aachen, was boren with just a head and mossy mane. He jorney'd the contrey, lonely, on his makeshift crook'd cornstalk legges, greeting tounefolk with his gastli grin. God forgeve them, they made every effort to drive hym away or tear him asunder. Near Deth was he when he dragg'd himself into my gardyn laberinthe, his cornstalk legges collaps'd. The moment I saw his toothey smyle and brass-button eies I knew the stabbe of Mortel love. It was as if I had inhal'd an hundrid of violets. Still, as I tended his wounds, I felt Wrathe once again over the violense he had suffr'd.

Poor Gryffix had no means to walke. Sory he was. I fashioned him a paire from willowe twigs. Never had I such passion and joi as the day my Gryffix and I could danse a reel! *Dere Rommi,* he called me, always tendre, always assayling me with fart japes and riddels, he sent me into hopeless giggels. I was and am still devoted to hym.

As you myghte gesse, I was downegraded fro' my Seintehood, the happiest day evere in my lyf. The tounefolk destruy'd the monument of me sitten in the High Towre of Heven and threw the bricks off the chalke clyffs of Rügen Ile. I and Gryffix live blysfully in our hous in marshe contrey. I am Erthly now, and the Hevens are naught but clouds that bring the gentel rains.

Artwork: *Blue Veiled Woman,* by Chaïbia Talal

BITTER QUEENS AND FOUNDLINGS

Miss Apples circles the town like a bird in its finery. A moon-faced woman, eyes blue as marbles, her speech as if all prepositions have slid from her basket.

May I buy an apple? I ask her, *A Saturn?*

She combs abandoned apple orchards, searching for Bitter Queens and Foundlings. Wild with the wild. Sometimes she rides past on an ancient bicycle, its big wheels creaking on the dusty path and searches for broken things left at the roadside. The children run after her or throw rocks. They call her a witch.

No Saturn. I only Jupiter today. She stares at me from light years away. They say she can read your soul with one look in the eye.

You come me. I give different one, you follow.

A humble fairy-tale house, inside, old photos in frames: a young soldier with his fist aloft in a band of revolutionaries; the portrait of a beloved leader, long gone.

This my daughter, Jenny Beauty. Apple name.

The daughter, eyes as bright as stars, sits in a wheelchair, red mouth in the shape of an 'O'. Her mother touches the top of the girl's head, whispers in a language like twigs scraping the wind. There is something electric between them. *Beauty give you apple.* The girl reaches into a deep, burgundy bowl. It has a large crack that's been mended.

"*Liberty*," the woman says. I cradle the apple. She smiles in a way she never has before. There's something of hunger about her—*and* abundance. How curiously these contraries play on her countenance.

I carry Liberty home. Place it on my windowsill, watch it cycle through the ripening days: maroon, dark red, blackish red. The skin becomes wrinkled. I can't bear to eat it.

Artwork: *The Pillowman* (panel 2), Paula Rego, 2004

LOVE'S SEASON

I'm happy here, on the velvet of your heart. Sleep, you soft man.
The shifting sands will soon reclaim you. The woman at your
back is the wife your brain forgot. But her blue eyes persist,
stored in a memory drawer that is locked. Is beauty in death a
myth? Neither of you, my parents, mastered it. Final faces even a
mirror would turn from, as if your beautiful lives were wrenched
inside out. That is the terrible love. There is no point when
grief ceases. It is the high tide and the low. The rapids and the
shallows. The riptide, too. Father, I remember when you forgot
how to bathe. I washed your feet. I, the only one you would allow.
That is the humbling love. Love—the beginning of lonely. Which
leads to which? A lighthouse is lonely as it has the world's oceans
to search. *I am not demented,* you told the doctor. Your clock face
was blank because time no longer existed. You were already out
there, exploring the vast sea. Two months after you sailed, I had a
dream I was driving us in an unknown country. I was lost. I cried
like a child. And *you* comforted *me* because you had died. Love's
season is summer. There is so much sand.

Artwork: *Medea,* Zurab Janiashvili, 2011

FIRE DANCING IN THE DARK

After classes she hangs her laundry on the clothesline. Her waist-high underwear hides a mountain under late snow. When the wind blows, vine maple twigs finger her private underthings. On the outside she's frosty and mannered. Inflexible. The children call her Miss Hunt.

She organizes the traditional maypole dancing every summer, instructing the young girls how to weave gracefully around the long ribbons. At home, in secret, she dances the Martha Graham Medea solo in her bare feet. She saw it in 1947 in New York, age twenty-one. Before the fire. Before her career was savaged. First she practises the "cave turn," a swooping heads-down spin in arabesque penché with a torso contraction. Then she practises other angular, forceful moves that don't exist in the classical ballet she teaches—dance that showcases beauty.

The little girls in her classes try her patience. Their pliés look as if they're squatting to sit on the toilet. They trip over their own feet as if their feet aren't attached to their body. What she hates most is their innocent pink faces.

She lives alone in a house with no mirrors. In the woods near the horse stables. Tonight is the "performance." In her home dance studio, in a red clinging dress, she opens the curtains to the outside world. Puts the record on: Samuel Barber, *Cave of the Heart*, a One-act Ballet. The Sorceress, cleansed by fire. She takes her hair out of its tight ponytail.

stiffly shaking as if consumed by emotion

from top of dress, pulls out long red ribbon, as if removing her viscera

looks fearfully at ribbon, yanks it as if in self-punishment

tosses ribbon away, jerky death throes, psychosis

crawls to it, crumples in ball, appears to eat it, throws up

does a demented angular tango

ribbon now attached to her navel, whiplashes herself, runs offstage...

Two of her former ballet students are hiding in the bushes outside, spying. They're frightened of her, with her burnt face and arms and stern way of speaking. They quit last month when they decided ballet wasn't "cool." When they felt curves reshaping their leotards. When they detected electricity emanating from boys, strange emotions overtaking their bodies. But tonight, in the dark, they stay and watch.

Photograph: *Who Was Dr. Halley? Three vintage diving helmets,*
Susan Smith, 2020

FREE DIVERS

There was nothing particularly eccentric about Mr. Chang. In
summer he wore green flip-flops and carried his library shopping
bag. In winter he wore his blue parka and carried his library
shopping bag. On the occasion of his death, things looked a little
different.

In town, his wife, a woman of changeable moods, was known as
Mrs. Chang, not surprisingly. (However, no one detected that
she was South Korean, not Chinese.) She was a fit woman with
a round nose, ordinary-enough clothes, but a seemingly catholic
taste in shoes. No flip-flops for her—except at her thrice weekly
swim regimen. The swimming public noted, on those occasions,
that she had a remarkable capacity for swimming an entire lane
underwater without ever taking a breath. Mr. Chang had married
Mrs. Chang late in life, after he retired in Gold Falls.

Just before he collapsed in the garden, Mr. Chang had called 911
and said, *I believe I am expiring.* When the police got through the
door they passed three different pairs of ladies' sandals. One,
white leather and practical. One vertiginously iridescent. And
the third an elegant crimson pair. There were three ladies' jackets
hanging from pegs, all the same. Passing the kitchen, the two
police officers saw a table set for four. On the wall, a browned
photo of three women sitting by the sea, wearing bathing caps. In
the bedroom, on the very large bed, four pillows.

A few years back, the town drunk, Jock, had knocked on Mr.
Chang's front door, asking for empty pop bottles. The door—he

claimed—was answered by three Mrs. Changs. Three identical Mrs. Changs. People laughed at his drunken delusion. Thereafter, Jock was followed everywhere by the taunt, *Seeing triple today?*

All the procedures regarding death were followed. The workshop was discovered. It was here that Mr. Chang, formerly a mechanical engineer, collected and repaired vintage medical, nautical and avionic apparatuses. Also three of everything. Among them: three antique phrenology calipers placed around the heads of three female busts; three circa 1870 antique gynecological instruments with silver fittings and porcupine quill shafts; and three B-17 ball turret azimuth position indicators.

His last project was on the bench. He had started it a year ago after the triplet sisters had gone back to Cheju, South Korea, to train a new generation of female free divers.

On the bench were three replica late seventeenth-century diving helmets. Inside each of the helmets was the face of one of his wives—identical, but not entirely. Although Styrofoam was not a forgiving medium, Mr. Chang accorded each sister her true visage. Jin Ah had the slight upturn at the left corner of her mouth; Sun Ah had heavier, dreamier eyelids; and Min Ah had the most serious expression: a grief-stricken brow.

Leaning against the wall opposite the bench was a complete vintage diving suit. Grinning through the glass panel of the diving helmet was a replica face of Mr. Chang.

Artwork: *Little Island,* by A.J. Casson, 1965

WHERE A DARK HEART BURNS

I move forward facing backward. Water drips from the oar tip.
There are those of us for whom islands are exile. For others
they're an oasis from humanity, where one can occupy oneself in
seclusion. *Sometimes you have to go dead to be alive again,* as she
put it, sequestering on this little island in an old shack built by an
artist.

In the distance, a woodpecker rams a tree with its beak. Fish
ribbon past under the lake's surface. They have names like walleye
and smallmouth, which imply something about why she wants to
be here. To look slant, to speak little.

She's dressed in white sack cloth. Shapeless. We step around the
poison oak. An outdoor table is set for three.

Company coming, love? I say.

She slits her eyes at me. *This is Effy.*

A sedge-woven thing. Sitting there on a cedar stump chair. Moss
hair, its eyes ghostly snowberries. Twig hands splayed as if stuck
in supplication. Straw child. *Our daughter,* she says, crazy hair
exploding from her head. I never knew my wife could carve. Or
weave. No words form in my mouth. Teacups filled, we eat white
cake in silence.

Are you coming home at some point? I ask.

You mean going home?

Well, either.

We're burning Effy first. Tonight.

Her soul seems to catch fire, too. Like old man's beard near a lit match. And when at the ashes stage she cries, I cry, too. From the northern reaches of the lake a loon pulls down the moon with its three-pitch lament.

I can no longer look to her to see myself. And yet I love her more now than before.

Artwork: *The Dream (The Bed)*, by Frida Kahlo, 1940

BECAUSE I AM SO OFTEN ALONE

I dissimulate sleep like a hesitating heart burrowing deep into singular. How fewer breaths are needed before the bone man appears with his thin arms full of wilting lilies, legs loaded with dynamite? Would the charge momentarily wake me? I will give you my eyes if you withdraw your unfleshed hands. You are not my canopy, nor I your corpse. My corset is metal, and yours is bone. I can open mine, you cannot. There's a copse somewhere in my mind's making while I mend, where creepers re-weave the body's wiring, re-leaving nerves into branchlets that reach back into life. My four posts are trees, and post-trees, supporting this thought: I'll be reborn into colour posthumously.

Artwork: an unattributed pseudo-vintage photo of a spectacled man with his head in a frame, in a suit, riding an ostrich with one square pasted-on eye

THE TOWN TALE OF DR. WEEP

I was out of my mind. Nothing left but flecks and fragments. I called on Dr. Weep, who had, by some sleight of hand, trapped his head in a TV screen. I found him in Newell Park patrolling on his ostrich whose eyes were paper cutouts. *Dr. Weep,* I implored him. *I've lost my mind.*

To which he responded, *If you would only put on a suit like me you would be more respected. You're ridden with shame of your inadequacies.*

Why do you ride an ostrich? I asked.

Because the more absurd I am, the less able people are to judge me, the more they revere me.

So, should I be absurd, too?

Of course not. You're an artist, not a professional! Then he rode off, framed head held high, his mount's black plumes bouncing convincingly like a can-can dancer's storied rump.

A long time ago, Dr. Weep was born Walter Deep. Raised in the low country where people pride themselves on the depth of their wells. Every night, his mother Margery put him to bed in a little wooden bucket and lowered him into the dark cone of the well. This was no cruelty. It was to protect him from bears that roamed the town of Penumbra. Little Wally slept well down there and had dreams of diving the vast, dark seas, or drilling long tunnels into limestone hills. At night, the well walls trapped small winds that swirled in the dark like Dervishes. Later, unsurprisingly, he had a knack for digging deep into the heart of things. One day, long after his bucketed past, he met a girl, Llewellyn. She had steely panther eyes, and a neck like an ostrich—long, elegant, with an alluring bend like a kitchen sink drain. He probed her up, down and all around, but she refused to yield to his affections. Wally Deep had fallen in love with the shallowest person in the county. He went mad from love, staining his fingertips yellow from weaving buttercup bracelets, writing love lyrics that made his eyes well up. He sent her dozens of scowling self-portrait photos made in the serious style of Daguerre himself. She sent them all back, frames and all. On the back of the last portrait she'd rejected, she wrote in chicken-scratch script, "Never, ever, will I kiss a man as absurd as you!"

You see him on Wellington Avenue each day, now older, single, with his TV frame head and bemused melancholy look, riding his ostrich with the dust mop plumes. The town children adore him. And, oddly, the citizens of Penumbra treasure his advice. Is he really a doctor? No one remembers. They come to him, broken, with their deepest, darkest woes and somehow Dr. Weep welds them back together again.

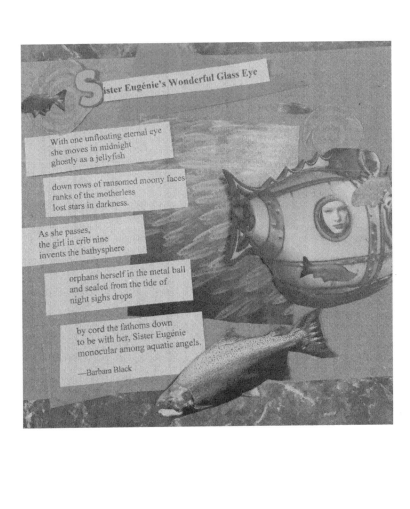

Sister Eugénie's Wonderful Glass Eye

With one unfloating eternal eye
she moves in midnight
ghostly as a jellyfish

down rows of ransomed moony faces
ranks of the motherless
lost stars in darkness.

As she passes,
the girl in crib nine
invents the bathysphere

orphans herself in the metal ball
and sealed from the tide of
night sighs drops

by cord the fathoms down
to be with her, Sister Eugénie
monocular among aquatic angels,

—Barbara Black

ANCESTRAL FABRICATIONS

CHILD BRIDE, HAWKESBURY, ONTARIO, 1918

Mother. A September apple. Conical, elongated, medium in size, yellow background, bright red mottling, as cheeks can be. Bears fruit when young. Perfumed flesh—when ripe. The old apples that still pass lips are: *Lady.* Tender flesh, fruit of aristocrats. *Mann. Maiden Blush. Knobbed Russet*—ugh. Potato-pocked, ugly welts and knobs. There is *Seek-no-Further.* It hangs on the tree until overripe. All the while, Mother is stripping an apple, a pale green eye. The toes of her boots laden with layers of peel. Lies upon lies upon. *You will sleep together in a bed as big as the moon, so big you can never reach the other side*, she says. The knife sweeps round and round, skinning the eye. I would not. I took to the cellar, the ripening room. Above, the season sloughed, rabbits flushed white to match the snow. Breathe. Cellar gas. Breathe. What other things are heavier than air? Unwilling womb shedding velvet; hope boiled dry in a cast-iron pan. Breathe. In the dark he will whisper to me *My dear you are like a lamp in the night.* Ethylene, kerosene, the names of lost girls. He will be *Wolf River* sweeter in the cold, roots solid on the shores of Lake Erie. I'll climb into his crown, make darkness my blanket. A captive heart must sleep with one eye open.

GRANNY LAROCQUE, 1892, RUSSELL, ONTARIO

Us girls ran the other way when we saw Granny Larocque
stomping out the back, screen door whacking the house
like a punishment, her eyes two pie slits, huge bosom a hot
broiling oven, apron strings flailing at her hips like the arms of
drowners and did she yell? no, did she swear? well, yes, she said
goddamhimgodalmightysonofa and the ground shrunk away from
her feet, chickens squawked crazy, and Gramp's favourite Miss
Pinkham blasted into the coop like walloped by a wind storm,
hunkered in the corner, quiet as goose down. Granny Larocque
she was small and had hands that could count your ribs even
with your sweater on and fingers like talons, not long, but wicked
skilled. She plucked Miss P right out, wrung her neck like a dish
cloth, chopped the head clean off and nailed it with the milk bill
to the door of Grandpa Frank's shack, ripped her apron right in
half, flung it on his front step, went back inside with her hair all
in curlers made her look like some old-town Medusa. Her hands
shook which they never did. Cob Brown snuck out the back of
the shack, bottle sloshing inside his jacket, and us Larocque girls
jumped into bed, tucked ourselfs in tight as two matches in a
matchbox, red heads sticking out like lit-up tinder.

DARK BY THE CRASHING DARK: FRANCOIS XAVIER LAROCQUE

An erasure of "The Battle of Lundy's Lane," Duncan Campbell Scott, (1916)

I

Yes, dig the furrow. Just sixteen but I didn't think—I, at the hill as the night broke,

guns sloped, devils the flag drove, until fierceness, slack dark, charged like a lion. Night cries the roar of a great angel. Yes, the strangest lightning you couldn't see—firing and

still; something, a strange noise thunder before us, the field, sullenly heavy, men and fire rage; distant clouds red.

II

My strange pain again piercing cold; old time alone would take more than you saw with your eyes. Oh! never say this: *a little boy, hair white as glorious God*—He was No God in Lundy's Lane.

LAST PINHOLE TO THE WORLD

Every day with his telescoped eye he watches, a sea-slapped window his frame. Some townsfolk here drink themselves into amnesia, favouring the brine of the pickled brain. But he drinks himself to clarity, until the blue slash of sky strips film from his eyes. Fluency is his domain. Ove has mastered the flotsam and jetsam of his mind. His religion? Riding the tides of his solitary existence. He doesn't believe in synchronicity or serendipity or any of those ipity-icities that posit you at the centre of the universe's perverse inclinations. But today is different. He had fixed the telescope on something long and large and shiny near the lighthouse. Something that had floated up. Fish, like people, come up only to die, as if light is a cure for mortality. And all Ove's life, fish found him, as they did Saint Botvid, that bastard missionary whose skull found a use for an axe.

It's six o'clock. The shimmering fish has reached the shore. He goes down to look. *Jätte sill!* A giant herring! Last seen in his grandfather's time. Could be as old as himself. They live down there, three thousand feet, far below the reach of any human eye. All pearl essence and undulating, scales flashing like a rainbow lighthouse. The silver makes him think of a battered tin toy he'd had as a boy, of his father smelling of gasoline, his mother crying into her cup, of time passed, when you could still hook up answers from the bottom of the sea. He kneels down beside the fish. Sixteen-foot long, tapered, floating in the wash like a fresh strip of steel. Finless, one eye gazing up, still seeing. A last pinhole to the world. He weeps as if it were a lost relative. Sentience, she has. He can feel it. He's convinced she's a she. He returns her gaze. It's the first tender moment of his life. But the moment she enters it, she leaves. Her waistless body, tattered and frayed, goes still. Light strikes her iridescent as he sits by her side until twilight green pulses like seawaves in the firmament, her one shining eye open to the sky.

THE JAEGER FAMILY THEATRE

You can't make a theatre only from the letter "T." My mother's last words. She sits up, flutters her hands into a long-tailed jaeger and wings her way back to Stekenjokk, where the light holds on through to midnight like a lamp left on just for you. All things felt can never be unfelt.

My ancestors were hunters and hunted: Jaegers. Stalked over generations by a fox deity who hid among granite boulders. Still, they flourished. Our theatre was built on this tundra and by theatre I mean our lives. They are one and the same. I want to tell my mother that for once I've written a story that's not sad. It sounds like yellow bells inside a shell being lulled by the outgoing tide. It is too late. We all enter the world green and vivid, climbing vine and grasping. We're bliss, bone, fusion, dissolution. In the end, our body migrates, but we leave our story behind. Our Jaeger Family T-h-e-a-t-r-e was built with all seven letters. Two parents and five children. Picture this: I'm onstage, dressed in jaeger plumage as the letter "T," my debut as the fifth born. Mother strings up lights, fastens her blue ribbons to my hair. Father's sinewy arms are cranking the curtain up. My father said I was born with eyes as tiny as salmonberry seeds. He himself was hazed with an etched-blue aura that followed him everywhere. All men in his family had one, except Anders. When Uncle Anders threw himself off the horizon, my grandmother said *Madmen are only as mad as men can be. Madwomen are as close to goddesses as a mortal can get.*

The curtain now shows me from the feet up, a *Stercorarius longicaudus* with a long, elegant tail and a human face. In our theatre, the wind was our only stage effect. Mother's blue hair ribbons unfurl like strips of sky. I sing the song I've been given: *Kreeahhh...* It travels far in the breeze, over the velvet green plateau.

SISTER EUGÉNIE'S WONDERFUL GLASS EYE

With one unfloating eternal eye she moves in midnight, ghostly
as a jellyfish, down rows of ransomed moony faces, ranks of the
motherless, lost stars in darkness.

As she passes, the girl in Crib Nine invents the bathysphere,
orphans herself in the metal ball and sealed from the tide of
night sighs drops by cord the fathoms down to be with her, Sister
Eugénie, monocular among aquatic angels.

HERRING RADIO

Waves licked the floorboards of his harbour hut as he sat, one ear cocked to the herring news, the other ear to the future, where waves slapped the shore of an unknown land. The man, untrusting of dialogue, never spoke to women, only sheep. *All women will come to us out of our need,* he said, and she one day stepped right out of the coffee can, full-grown and arms that could snap his spine, eyes shining and milky like oysters.

This is how he told it.

This is how it was.

She was descended from a herring down Marstrand way. A large willful girl with silvery eyes, magnetism that pulled like North Sea tides. Sinewy men dreamed of her net-hauling arms, plunged deep into carcasses, pulling out a heart—theirs. She'd lived up there longer than him, eating dried flounder and dulce, years measured in skeins of wool carded from sheep that strayed her way, spun to the falling of month-long snows, knitted into men. Which she threw into the sea. Except that one—that was him.

FEVER, N-GONG HILLS, GREAT AUNT CALLA, 1953

Rhinos thrash rushes, rattling the air. The great plain licks
wounds into malarial flames. Polyglot death rasps the grassy
chants, syllabling her pillowed ear. From the parlor her husband
at the untuned piano, a dirge in Db minor scything every nerve.
Dazzling light drips down in strands. A Kikuyu man enters in a
whispering gown: *Memsahib, I will put out the ancient fires.* In the
embers of her mind, psalms she remembers from Gothenburg:
But You, O LORD, are a shield around me...

Old Kikuyu god Ngai peels back the hills. She crawls out,
blackened. It is the end of the withering season. Yet, in the
darkness: silent machetes.

WHAT SHE HEARD AS MUSIC

It was inside the old farmhouse, inside walls, composing in
between the wood grain gaps, inside lacewings in May, in pike in
the shallows, inside the water that was inside their gills. It was
inside stag antlers, vibrating the velvet, inside owl eyes scanning
for mice, in the heads of lice, and the mallet striking spike with
iron intent. Inside all things hidden and forbidden. In the body
of the fiddle that was thrown to the fire. It was mother with a
knife and father with a saw, the flesh of lamb, the flesh of oak,
the loam and the ice, the cracking and the healing, the lake
that sighed when the sun died red, and in lightning that singed
the lit-up hills. In fireflies in jars, in the baby bird's mouth, and
secrets buried in the yard. Then. Mother trapped it in a trunk
and sealed it with tape. Destination: Lynchburg, Virginia. That
night, Grace prayed to the crescent moon. Sisters waved goodbye
in the morning grey. First train took her to a woman with a voice
like rain, who caressed her head, saying, *Child, you will sing again.*
There was no music—even unheard—that God did not invent.
When the girl opened the bulging trunk, all the world's yearning
and her voice flowed out.

FRANCOIS XAVIER LAROCQUE: METHOD FOR THE AFTERLIFE

They buried the Grand Old Methodist at Van Cleek Hill,
Ontario, in the rain, his heart collapsed like an overripe pear. He
was grand. And he was old. But, unknown to many, he was no
longer a Methodist, except for the meticulous daily grooming
of his prophet-like beard and the care with which he ushered
his livestock through life to death. His method, considered
unorthodox at the time, was to speak to them as he carried out
his tasks, and in the evening when they settled into their stalls, he
sat on a milking stool and read to them from La Fontaine's Fables.

It was 1883 when he departed. Confident in the afterlife he had
dreamed for himself, having glimpsed the dispassionate force
from which we must extract our necessary truths. *We men are
animals too,* was his maxim. Not wishing to endure resurrection,
he unpacked his skull—he liked to go light. He left behind his
old skin and the musket bullet in his leg to enter the underworld
of his own creation. This was the method. While his daughters
blew prayers into their handkerchiefs, while his nephew scraped
Un Canadien Errant on his apple crate fiddle and the widow
Larocque hunched in the rain like a question mark, he was on a
journey through clay and earth. While the minister threw ashes
as if seasoning a stew, Larocque moved through loam like a man
become worm, became soil and substrate, past protozoans and
pauropods, actinomycetes and rotifers, an immigrant to the
underworld, while those above gasped in the thin air of a cosmos
less one man with a beard.

ARTHUR ALEXANDER FINDS HIS MÉTIS WIFE, 1897

The sun wasn't the sun it was before. This sun made him
transparent. The whole world shone through him. He was a
magnifier moving in a vividness. He practised, all along the
Dawson Road, making love to the palm of his hand, never fearing
the loss of his magnitude. If he could have, he would have slept
standing up. His heart was—his whole body was his heart.
He was master of rough yearning, breathing in each burning
night, rushing headlong into the new century, his body a steam
engine crashing the future. He found you. In St. Boniface in the
machinery of dawn. *Edna*, he said, hands hot on your shoulders
as he leaned his tall frame into yours, tongue a strip of tinder.
Your slap was the sound of a trunk split by lightning. Already
you contained the daughter he would send away and the son
who would flee and the charge that would trigger a fire and burn
down the forest of your complicated love.

Love is a pitch too high for the human ear, the hissing of
a spruce's burning core. Still, he caressed the sting of your
handprint on his face.

MOTIVELESS UNDER THE ORANGE EYE

She hangs, in her original sinless way, a live green coil in a mango tree. No one sees her, except for *Now*. River moves, motiveless under the orange eye. Smell sparks her forked tongue—an image forms inside her mouth. Air's weight shifts to ambush. She darts. She swallows: bird... fire finch. Reorders its cellular map. This is a talent she has. Her body is her brain. She never wonders or wants, only inhabits her skin—each one. When *Now* turns the day black with silver holes, it sends up *Serpens*, her starry sister. Under the large white eye, she sleeps, without knowledge, coffin-shaped head at rest. When she falls from the tree, her spine will become Woman.

EACH CELL OF YOUR BODY A TINY CLOCK

These last winter years. You forget how many. Your fingers forget the biting chill. Things hide under banks of snow. Night is day and day is night. The downstairs room, everything strewn in pieces: crystals, clock hands, crowns, chimes, mainsprings unsprung. And pendulums. The stream of people at your door with broken clocks, watches stopped. You're well-known now. In your hallway cubbyhole you try to restore the works. But some things can't be fixed.

Forty years ago, you bought the canyon house. Did you choose the roaring creek or did it choose you? Water, always the background of your life. The flow, the anti-clock. The roar of the creek inside your head.

Remember 1929? The man was your father. Before he arrived, your mother's ghostly nightie, flailing on the clothesline. As if she were still inside it, struggling to get it off. Train calling from a distance. He was tall and contained. Your name is his. He'd come to look at you in your crib, the room as small as a closet. His blue eyes were yours. Like two Great Lakes. He left his pocket watch behind.

There are pendulums swaying, the weight of things that can't be undone, that continue to haunt you. It bothers you that you can't remember the man's voice.

It was hot. The crying children. The clock hand stuck at eight o'clock. It'd been like that for years, its duty to tell time no longer honoured. The Red River was low that summer, stones exposed that had never been seen. The previous year, it was so deep and swift several children had drowned. Time is a river—in a way.

A RECIPE

You start with love, then you fry a fish. I know you can't see
how the two go together, but they do. You start with the hairs
on the back of a man's neck. You may not believe this, but
the connection depends on those few tiny hairs which lie like
filaments in waiting, primed for the electric moment. If the sun
shines, you see them, lined up, their shafts illuminated, their tips
curved ever so slightly. Touch this spot on a man's neck and the
world shrinks to one fingertip on one hair, a microcosmic charge.
This is how it begins. Devotion, its pale cousin, comes later.

Take two fresh fish. Batter. Drop in a fry pan of sizzling oil. If
you're lucky, you'll hear the souls whistling their way back to
their watery source. Once cooked, salt plentifully and slide onto a
large oval platter, with their hot eyes glistening.

Later, you find yourself frying fish and crying at the bones,
pulling out the translucent slivers. You fry the fish because he
offered it across a frozen river that now separates you. Somehow,
he hooked it from under the ice. He is resourceful. He sits at
the table, waiting to be served. When the fish, fried and crispy,
appears in front of him with its glossy eyes, he leans back and
rubs his hands on the back of his neck. He doesn't know that he
does this. But that's the connection. That's what's left of it.

As If the Outline of a Country Had Appeared On My Face
Notes from the Maasai Mara

The stars have rearranged themselves
without my knowing.

Each night, the moon
a quarter slice of pink.

Thorns dream flesh.

"There's a fragrance like lilies,"
I say, but no one else can smell it.

I dream versions of myself I don't like.
My friend, who is not my friend, says,

"You are not who you say you are!"

There is no difference between
hiding and dying a little death.

—Barbara Black

DISORIENTATIONS

KNOWING HOW TO FIND THE END

A humid night, Genoa, July 1882. Nietzsche washes his face
twice, goes to bed and dreams he's in a dimly lit ballroom. On the
dance floor a figure flexes wildly to flamenco. Nietzsche swings a
kerosene lamp to see the face, but it's unfixed, ever-shifting like a
fire. The figure spins, raises its arms as if clasping a sun. Nietzsche
joins the dance, his body cycling through fluidity, defiance,
passion. In the background the beat of fingers slapping palms:
tà-ca-ta-ca, tà-ca tac.

Do you know who I am? Nietzsche shouts over the music.

Yes, of course! I created you! says the figure.

That is incorrect. This is my dream.

I created that, too, the figure says, stomping out a series of rapid
zapateado.

Tà-ca-ta-ca, tà-ca tac...

I've never been so happy, Nietzsche cries, foot tapping lightning-
fast. *Am I dead?* he asks the figure, leaning toward it.

Yes, of course. As am I—thanks to you. The figure explodes in a
flash of green light. Crystal shards scatter across the floor. Palms
smack palms: *tà-ca-ta-ca, tà-ca-ta-ca...*

1888. Turin. Nietzsche holds a mirror up to his face and combs
his commanding moustache, careful to hide the gentle man
underneath. He retires to bed and sleeps fitfully as carriages

clatter over cobblestones in the night. He dreams that his moustache has broken away from him and gone to join the face of a dictator. It sits now on this rigid face, not unlike a domesticated panther whose regular meals keep it from ravaging its host. It has become more famous than him. Soon it will be promoted to Minister of Culture and tout the nationalist merits of Wagnerian opera. It will crave the sound of jackboots pounding pavement.

1889. Basel. Nietzsche looks in the mirror. He sees Voltaire, Caesar and Napoleon. But not himself. He is escorted to bed on an evening of unrelenting hail. He dreams he's in an empty asylum at the piano, playing his piece *Albumblatt*. It's a concert, but without an audience. A minute and forty-five seconds into the piece there's a section with a repeated note. He gets stuck on it, hitting it repeatedly like a madman on a typewriter, then waits for the sound to decay. At some point he doesn't hear the pitch anymore, just an ever-expanding reverberation slow as the millennial shifting inside a granite block. After three days of this, he lifts his index finger off the key. A voice asks, "How does it feel, Herr Nietzsche, to perform in a country in which you are the only inhabitant?"

ADVICE WHILE STAYING IN THE MAASAI MARA

Sleep with one eye open. Keep the dreaming one open, not the other one. The dreaming eye is more tender, more observant, the more exuberant of the two. If a zebra comes, this may affect reception and require an application of electric stinging beetles. The dreaming eye will tell you that the zebra is a narcissist that requires five three-way mirrors to get dressed in the morning. Stripes are its vanity. The sleeping eye doesn't care. It exists in a world of horizontals and verticals. It can't even *see* a zebra for that reason. The dreaming eye goes into the scrubland searching for bands of mongoose to have a nine-way conversation in high pitches. So many things can happen under a moon shaped like a hammock. While the dreaming eye plunges into the watering hole in search of a hippo, the sleeping eye bores itself trying to connect stars into constellations named after Greek philosophers. Because it is asleep, it thinks itself a genius, but meanwhile the dreaming eye is looking down the hippo's throat to the place where the mud it consumed all day has reconfigured into a village for the drowned. Deep inside the huts, small fires sputter. The drowned are like dreamers, except they don't dream.

AS IF THE OUTLINE OF A COUNTRY HAD APPEARED ON MY FACE

Notes from the Maasai Mara

The stars have rearranged themselves without my knowing. Each night, the moon a quarter slice of pink. Thorns dream flesh. *There's a fragrance like lilies,* I say, but no one else can smell it. I dream versions of myself I don't like. My friend, who is not my friend, says, *You are not who you say you are!* At home my father becomes scrubland, mapless, a nomad of the mind, stepping in his own footprints from the day before without knowing they are his.

Sight vanishes with the light. There is no horizon. Hyenas launch strange arias from the grasslands. Through our pores we listen. We no longer have our language. Our stories have vanished. In our dreams, Maasais jump—*adumu*—up and down, up and down, as if launched by invisible pogo sticks. They smile. They know us more than we know ourselves. Red dirt builds under our fingernails. Our eyes have changed. Time is eerily elastic. On the highway a shrivelled man held a sign: *4 I know the plans I hav 4 you declares the lord.* A giraffe paced the highway's edge, terrified of crossing. We walk blindly to bed. Camp room doors close for the last time. We are once more contained. How gently the Maasai Mara guide had cut the goat's throat as if his knife were a lullaby.

I burst through the door of my childhood house. The house is expecting me. My mother is there, expecting me—like in theatre, coming onstage to face an actor in character. The story is in place. My mother is not just my mother; she's playing my mother and has that gathered calm of knowing. She's turned sideways, folding a towel. She doesn't look at me. Her body says *I know you. I know what happens in your subterranean world.* It's like a Pinter play. Is every child's story coded in a mother's womb before she gives birth?

I slip past her down the ugly carpeted hallway longer than in real life, a forced march toward judgment behind that door. Is my mother the witness or the judge? I don't open the door—instead, I open the closet door, lift the carpet to reveal the floorboards. This is always a bad sign in a dream. There are no loose boards.

My mother stands at the end of the hallway, watching. Mothers are never dead. Before being ushered to the afterworld, their particulates reconfigure to follow your exploits on earth.

Her eyes track my panicked search: I ransack drawers, tear open boxes, knock on walls. Have I committed a crime? The evidence must be hidden in the house. My mother knows the offense. My search becomes more desperate. A realization erupts from my bowels. It's not an innocent childhood crime, like breaking a vase or cutting holes in her towels. It's a grave crime. Have I killed someone? Is something buried? I may be searching not for a weapon but for evidence like a femur or ribs. An organ. My mother knows where this evidence is, a burden to carry throughout her life, but never her duty to reveal it. Is this why her body still lingers here—to protect or condemn me? She stands sentry, saying much by saying nothing. I try to remember the nature of her love.

KAFKA'S DREAM DIARIES

I

I find my seat on the overnight train to Leipzig. Fall asleep in minutes. Train stops, so assume it's Leipzig. No Max in sight. Step down drowsily to platform. Very odd. No further train tracks. Granular dust blows everywhere. Pointy, layered mountains under two moons. Unpeopled. Ah, my vain hope to escape the insurance reports, the hordes. Somewhere to be wrapped in blessed solitude! No sooner than this thought occurs, a stampede appears on the horizon. A moving organism, like a battalion of schoolboys when the grub bell rings, increasing in size to a huge crowd, waving banners and streamers and shouting *Hail the leader!* Not referring to me, it turns out. Max Brod, my great friend and literary executor appears, carried aloft in the crowd. Nude, on an opulent sedan chair. Emperor of the planet. Comes with a decree: *Franz Kafka is hereby rewarded with the task of building a Great Wall, stone by stone, around a Great Tower which itself will house every word he ever wrote. An honour!* A tomb. An exile of drudgery. Same life I had before. Only worse. Not a brothel in sight. Emperor Max says the Great Tower will be topped with an enormous, flashing, rotating "K" that will outshine all the other planets in the galaxy.

People are always less convincing without their clothes.

II

A grotty cabaret in the Jewish ghetto underneath a printer's shop. Cabaret Lucerna. Musty, dim. Cockroach coaches scuttle to and fro at my feet. Smoke from cigars and cigarettes fogs the stage, clogs the lungs. Flimsy curtain opens. Doctor Freud on stage dressed as Oedipus. Booms, *Father, O my father!*, addressing his cardboard dagger. Oversized costume slides awkwardly off his shoulders. Spare me the father fate, the wretched course of destiny. Where's my favourite actor Löwy? I escape to the backroom, which looks more like a courtroom and is full of carnivalists. A series of tables, each covered with a long white strip and drinking straws. *Come! Come join us*, says an unconvincing werewolf, leading me by the elbow. Patrons dressed in carnival costumes hunch over the white substance, place a straw in their nostrils and inhale it up their noses. *It's his latest. The Metamorphosis!* one of them says giddily. I scoop up a handful. Run it through my fingers. The white flecks are indeed shredded pages of my book. A shapely female skeleton approaches: *By ingesting the book in this manner, we believe that the author's words will be understood bodily rather than being merely read.*

An unholy host! They'll claim like everyone else to have read my work but, like everyone else, they haven't.

Books are a narcotic.
—Franz Kafka

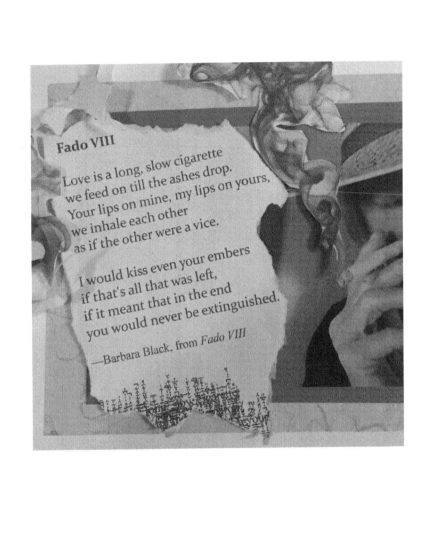

Fado VIII

Love is a long, slow cigarette
we feed on till the ashes drop.
Your lips on mine, my lips on yours,
we inhale each other
as if the other were a vice.

I would kiss even your embers
if that's all that was left,
if it meant that in the end
you would never be extinguished.

—Barbara Black, from *Fado VIII*

FADO

FADO I

Each love has its weight, its particular dream. Over time it dreads its own undoing. It dreads being stranded in a starless night. A star is an end, not a beginning. Lovers, you are untouched by grace because you have stopped believing in it. Now night comes, with its indecipherable prayer; a prayer come to kill you if only you would wake.

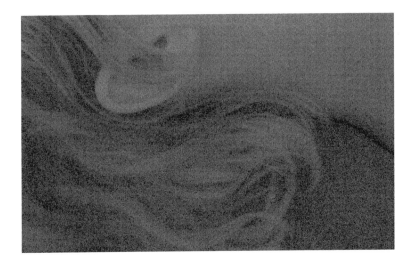

FADO II

God of the decaying note, why was I born like this, with a deep cut in my voice that never heals? I searched for signs. I heard sighs of the dead. On the backs of swans, I wrote down their songs. I tried to sing them and instead I wept. Our voice is and is not ours. I tore out the cords of my aching throat. But still they ask me for the broken songs.

FADO III

I won't speak of spring, nor of its salt breath. Remember how the tides poured across our bed? We floated to a strange country, fish like scrolls at our feet. The heart is... nothing we can see nor say, a dead sea without fury. You are a desert isle, dreaming drought. I wanted to live in that country but for want of water.

FADO IV

Life for me is to wander in a blind mist, to never grieve the dawn. The horizon is always distant. This way, I need no farewells. My dear heart, there is no lover for me. By walking, I fall in love with the world. I follow the footsteps of the god I myself have created.

FADO V

All things contain their future, once fulfilled, they depart. Inside me, an old song has rewritten itself. Once, I heard your body's notes and hid them in my violet wings. Together we lived on the thin light of dusk. But night came on with its hungry mouth. You left, tongue torn like a scarlet petal. Come to my garden, come back to me, let the nightingale embrace your silence. Live secretly inside my breast. Oh—your eyes have become roses, your hands the thorns.

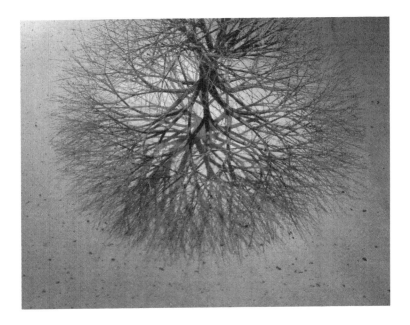

FADO VI

Memory is a rock smashed into pieces. I tell only the best parts, the sharpest fragments. That canyon of my childhood had an eye that never closed. You want me to say that the river was my lover, that I wore its water like a silky slip, that I loved its liquid voice, luxuriated in its sibilance.

Don't mistake that sound for love. Even now, every night, it's in my dreams. An eye in the dark, a voice speaks: *breasts like boulders, eyes like stones*—but I always resist.

FADO VII

Heart in a cage, heart laden with ice, heart the weight of a
paralyzed bird, heart that cannot float, heart in a stranger's
clothing, heart a rotted cross of wood, no one hears you in this
oblivious place. You were born in the midst of this torrent, a
collector of sleepless nights, your blood runs cold with minerals,
your cries are glacial silt. The eddy asks a question: *Can you hear
your name?* Love is dispersion, drop by drop.

FADO VIII

You stole my eyes. I learned to navigate the spaces between.
Echoes became etchings on my brain, distances the contours
of your face. Your breath changed into animal. We came to fear
light. In the dark we were flesh and feel, amplified by blindness.

FADO IX

When you cut me did I bloom red or blue? How do I hold my
sutured heart? Tell me why the blind have tranquil faces, why
your voice is like a sedative, why you always play the fugitive
jumping from a train. I am your phantom limb, bleeding an
amnesiac juice. Kiss me and the red taste of iron revives me.

FADO X

Love is a long slow cigarette we feed on until the ashes drop. Your lips on mine, my lips on yours, we inhale each other as if the other were a vice. I would kiss even your embers if that's all that was left, if it meant that in the end you would never be extinguished.

NOTES AND REFERENCES

DISTILLATIONS

PORT

Old Love references an Amália Rodrigues song, "Fado Português."

Lake Creatures references a Paula Rego artwork, *3 Faces do Medo*.

Fernando António Nogueira Pessoa Portugal's famous poet Fernando Pessoa wrote in over a hundred different alter egos, including Àlvaro de Campos, a naval engineer who in some ways surpassed Pessoa himself. After his death, Pessoa left behind thirty thousand pieces of paper in a trunk. *She would genuflect to tie his shoes* references Paula Rego's *The Cadet and His Sister*.

We No Longer Have to Whisper Name of the bar from Paula Rego's *O Corvo Noturno*. Portuguese Dictator António de Oliveira Salazar ruled the country from 1932 to 1968.

Everything Transfixed is based on a powerful dream I had at age six.

Bruised Mango *spit out the fire* references a Maria Teresa Horta poem, "Ponto de Honra"/ Point of Honour.

I Am Real references an Ana Luísa Amaral poem, "A mais perfeita imagem"/The Most Perfect Image." *I am real and you are not* is from a comment on real vs. pretend by Paula Rego in the art film *Telling Tales*.

GIN

Stitching is a micro-tribute of sorts to Virginia Woolf's *To the Lighthouse*.

Gotunabe is based on a Japanese mythological figure called Hitotsume-kozō, a supernatural apparition that takes on the appearance of a bald-headed child with one eye in the centre of its forehead.

Small Tenders The mysterious figure that emerges from the forest and appears to the younger woman is based on the Swedish folk creature, skogsrå or "forest spirit," who has the appearance of a beautiful woman when seen from the front, but from behind looks like a hollow tree trunk.

Just for the Record was inspired by the line "The Creator who dashed off a bird..." from poet Laura Kasischke's poem "The Accident."

The Transformation of Miss Emily Evans was adapted into a comic chamber opera, titled "The Transformation of Miss Emily Evans." Music by Katerina Gimon, libretto by Barbara Black. The work was commissioned by Erato Ensemble and premiered in June 2022.

The Bones of Amundsen has in mind artist Louise Bourgeois's giant spider sculpture called "Maman."

BOURBON

The Map of My Wanderings was sparked by a line in Lydia Davis's *Collected Stories*: "Mrs. D consults a doctor about her trouble conceiving," from the story "Mrs. D and Her Maids."

TEQUILA

Invisible Ink is based on an article in *The New York Times* about a protester in Kazakhstan, Aslan Sagutdinov, 22, who stood in a public square holding a blank sign, predicting he would be detained.

Tibicina Corsica Corsica was written on the island of Sardinia after I observed that there was an alarming dearth of bees and other pollinators amidst a plethora of blooming shrubs.

SCOTCH

The Angels Fall on a Day with No Rain is set in a town similar to the ruined town of Poggioreale in Sicily. Inspired by the photographic project called "The Sleepers" by photographer Elizabeth Heyert.

We Do Not Lie Down was written while listening to "Winter" from Piazzolla's *Four Seasons in Buenos Aires*, performed by Gidon Kramer, Kremerata Baltica.

RUM

What the Mouth Knows was partially influenced by Samuel Beckett's monologue *Not I,* in which a mouth speaks through a curtain, recounting a traumatic series of events.

WHISKEY

Observations from a Visit to the Museum of Saint Barbara was written using some structures of the Little Poetry Project, a prompt exercise developed by Jim Simmerman, taken from *The Practice of Poetry*, Robin Behn and Chase Twitchell, eds. Simmerman's purpose was to fracture logic and reach for the "sheer oddities of language itself."

On The Edges of Where We Live Lurk the Untitled Masterpieces of Our Dreams came from an exercise in a Meg Pokrass workshop on 50-word stories.

THE UNSEEN

What May Console Those with the Loss of Their Lexicon came about during a difficult, year-long bout of writer's block. It was written while listening to the album *Amina Alaoui, Arco Iris*, and especially listening to "Bùscate en Mì" (Seek Yourself Within Me), a poem by Saint Teresa of Avila.

Ink in a Dye Bath is based on a philosophical proposition by Frank Jackson called The Knowledge Argument. "The experiment describes

Mary, a scientist who exists in a black-and-white world where she has extensive access to physical descriptions of color, but no actual perceptual experience of color. [...] The central question of the thought experiment is whether Mary will gain new knowledge when she goes outside the colorless world and experiences seeing in color." (Wikipedia)

The Brothers Cisoires is an exercise in "object defamiliarization," an assignment from the 2023 flash fiction workshop "Open Your Art," hosted by master flashers Kathy Fish and Nancy Stohlman. The object being described is a pair of scissors ("cisoires" in old French).

My Tiny Life was inspired by a tiny wooden box with a tiny handwritten book inside which we found among my father's belongings after his passing.

VISUAL PROVOCATIONS

The Path to Inspiration references Nicole Eisenman's painting *Conscious Mind of the Artist (Subconscious Decision and Actions in Progress)* and her comment on artists "...it is our job to create something out of nothing." *Art Pulse: Nicole Eisenman: The Relevance of 21st-Century Expressionism* by Stephen Knudsen.

Daughter of the North Wind is an ekphrastic work based on a painting by American artist Kim Dingle, titled *Cloud*, 1999.

The Miraclous Ruine of Seinte Romhilde von Rothenburg arose from *Scivias, Vision XI: Vision of the Last Days*, an image by Hildegard von Bingen (before 1179), and is in no way related to the original content of that work. The language is a mash-up of Middle English dialects.

Bitter Queens and Foundlings was written after viewing *Blue Veiled Woman*, by Moroccan artist Chaïbia Talal, thanks to a workshop with Lorette Luzajik of *The Ekphrastic Review*.

Love's Season was inspired by the second panel in Paula Rego's triptych painting *Pillowman*, 2004, which itself was inspired by

Martin McDonagh's play, "The Pillowman." Rego stated that the pillow-like figure symbolized her father.

Fire Dancing in the Dark was the result of studying Zurab Janiashvili's painting *Medea*, 2011.

Free Divers was composed based on a photograph of three vintage diving helmets, taken by American photographer Susan Smith.

Where a Dark Heart Burns was influenced by A.J. Casson's painting, *Little Island*. Thanks to Vancouver Flash Fiction founder Karen Schauber for this inspiration.

Because I Am So Often Alone was inspired by *The Dream (The Bed)*, 1940, by Frida Kahlo.

The Town Tale of Dr. Weep was inspired by an unattributable fake vintage photo of a man with his head in a frame in a suit riding an ostrich that has a pasted-on eye. It lives on somewhere in the Internet universe.

ANCESTRAL FABRICATIONS

Child Bride is based on two ancestral sources. The first a reference to my ancestor Philibert Couilleau de Laroque who in 1676 took a thirteen-year-old girl Suzanne Catherine La Porte for his wife. The second source is a memory of my paternal grandmother's of fetching an apple from the cellar and watching her uncle slowly peel it. All apples mentioned are actual heritage apples.

Granny Larocque is a close recounting of an event described by my paternal grandmother Rose Larocque of her mother kicking her alcoholic father out of the house and making him live in a shack in the backyard (and insisting he still pay the milk bill!).

Dark by the Crashing Dark is an erasure of Canadian poet Duncan Campbell Scott's poem "The Battle of Lundy's Lane" (1916) concerning the War of 1812. The Battle of Lundy's Lane, fought on July 25, 1814, between an invading American army and a British-Canadian army near present-day Niagara Falls, Ontario, was one of the deadliest battles fought in Canada. My paternal great-grandfather Francois Xavier Larocque fought in this war as a young man.

Last Pinhole to the World is based both on my imagined Swedish/Norwegian ancestry (maternal) and on a newspaper article which described a Swedish man's discovery of a rare *Regalecus glesne* (giant herring or oarfish).

The Jaeger Family Theatre is an imagining of my maternal Nordic ancestry and the possibility that I am descended from the (fictitious) jaeger bird people.

Sister Eugénie's Wonderful Glass Eye was inspired by my paternal grandmother's stay in the St. Boniface orphanage in Winnipeg when her brother Frankie was born.

Herring Radio is a fanciful fabrication of how my maternal great-grandfather and grandmother may have come to be. However, there really is such thing as herring radio.

Fever, N-Gong Hills, Great Aunt Calla, 1953 describes a malarial episode in my maternal Great Aunt Calla's life as a 35-year ex-pat living in Nairobi and references the Mau Mau uprising. Ngai (also called Múrungu or Enkai) is the monolithic Supreme God in the spirituality of the Kikuyu (or Gikuyu) people of Kenya. Psalm 3: Deliver Me, O LORD! (2 Samuel 15:13–29).

What She Heard as Music was inspired by a tiny piece of information: that one of my Norwegian maternal great-grandmother's siblings, a sister named Lavinia Nillson, was given away to adoption and became a famous singer. This piece was also inspired by the movement, "Verano/Summer" from Piazzolla's *Four Seasons of Buenos Aires*, original recording.

Francois Xavier Larocque: Method for the Afterlife reimagines the moment of my paternal great-great-grandfather's burial in East Hawkesbury, Ontario, and journey to the afterlife. I inherited an apple box fiddle made by a family member from my grandmother Larocque.

Arthur Alexander Finds His Métis Wife is based on a true account of my paternal great-grandfather running away from Thunder Bay to the Dawson Trail (Ontario) to find his love, my grandmother's mother, Edna Pearl Walker, who was believed to be Métis.

Motiveless under the Orange Eye Mambas were a feature of my maternal Great Aunt Calla's property in Nairobi, often seen in trees in her creekside garden or under the deck stairs.

Each Cell of Your Body a Tiny Clock Almost nothing is known about my father's natural father. Here I imagine the moment when he came to Transcona, Manitoba, to see his out-of-wedlock son who in later life became a watchmaker.

A Recipe is a purely imaginary scene of my maternal great-great-grandmother and grandfather in Norway.

DISORIENTATIONS

Knowing How to Find the End The title is excerpted from Friedrich Nietzsche's *The Gay Science*, 124:3, 480. "Knowing how to find the end.... Masters of the very first order can be recognized by the following characteristics: in all matters great and small they know with perfect assurance how to find the end, whether it be the end of a melody or of a thought, whether it be the first act of a tragedy, or the end of a political action."

Advice While Staying in the Maasai Mara is influenced by a line by Surreal artist Leonora Carrington, "The task of the right eye is to peer into the telescope while the left eye peers into the microscope."

Your Subterranean World is based on a dream I had in Laveno Mombello, Lago Maggiore.

Kafka's Dream Diaries After his death, Kafka left behind a collection of writings which he asked to be burned by his assigned executor, his friend Max Brod. Brod did not comply. The second dream is dedicated to *Vancouver Sun* book reviewer Tom Sandborn, who, in his review of my short story collection *Music from a Strange Planet*, coined the irresistible compliment: "Think Kafka on crack."

FADO

Fado is a deeply felt form of Portuguese music that inspired my fado stories. The unique poetry of fado is based on common themes: Lisbon (or other places) anthropomorphized; nostalgia; grief; voice; destiny; betrayal or loss in love. And *saudade*, a yearning for the unattainable.

PUBLICATION AND AWARDS

Heartfelt gratitude to publications and contests that have published my work. Some are previous versions of those in this collection.

DISTILLATIONS

PORT

We No Longer Have to Whisper Second Prize, James Joyce Bloomsday Short Fiction Contest, 2016

Everything Transfixed Published in *What Can't Be Contained*, Leaf Press 2014

GIN

Stitching Nominated for VERA Flash Fiction Award by *The Cincinnati Review* 2020; Published, *Cincinnati Review*, miCRo series, 2020

Gotunabe Nominated for Microfiction of the Year by *The Cincinnati Review* 2019; Published, *Cincinnati Review*, miCRo series, 2020

Just for the Record Finalist, *The Ekphrastic Review*, Bird Watching Contest, May 2021

The Transformation of Miss Emily Evans Transformed into a comic chamber opera with libretto by Barbara Black and music by Katerina Gimon, premiered in June 2022 by Erato Ensemble

The Bones of Amundsen Longlisted, *PRISM* Grouse Grind Contest 2020 (Very Short Forms)

BOURBON

Mount Pedernal at Sunrise Longlisted, Bath Flash Fiction Award 2020; Published in *Bath Flash Fiction Award Anthology Five 2020, Restore to Factory Settings*

Crgizl Winner, *Geist* 15th Annual Literary Postcard Story Contest 2019; Published in *Geist*, Issue 113, Summer 2019

Barker's Quality Wood Floor Cream Shortlisted, 2023 Edinburgh Award for Flash Fiction; Published in *Scottish Arts Trust Story Awards*, Volume 5, November 2023

The Map of My Wanderings Winner, Federation of BC Writers Literary Contest, 2022; Published in *FBCW Literary Contest Volume 2*

TEQUILA

Tibicina Corsica Corsica Published in *Prairie Fire*, Special Issue "House on Fire," 2020

SCOTCH

The Angels Fall on a Day with No Rain Longlisted, New Writers Flash Fiction Competition 2022

We Do Not Lie Down Winner, Federation of BC Writers Literary Contest 2021 (Flash Fiction); Published in *Roots to Branches*, Volume 1

THE UNSEEN

Lowercase Sisters Shortlisted, Federation of BC Writers, Literary Contest 2021 (Flash Fiction); Published in *FBCW Literary Contest Volume 2*; Longlisted, *PRISM* Grouse Grind Contest 2020 (Very Short Forms)

Ink in a Dye Bath Shortlisted, The Plaza Prizes International Competition 2023 (Flash Fiction); Published in *The Plaza Prizes Anthology 1*

Fishboy Published in *Fracture*, Leaf Press, 2016

Where Women Go in Middle Age Published in *Rockvale Review*, Issue Two, 2018

VISUAL PROVOCATIONS

The Miraclous Ruine of Seinte Romhilde von Rothenburg Longlisted, Federation of BC Writers Literary Contest 2022 (Flash Fiction)

Bitter Queens and Foundlings Longlisted, Federation of BC Writers Literary Contest 2022 (Flash Fiction)

Fire Dancing in the Dark Longlisted, Smokelong Grand Micro Competition 2023 (Flash Fiction)

Where a Dark Heart Burns Winner, Vancouver Flash Fiction, Prompt No. 7, 2020; Featured Flash, Miramichi Flash, *The Miramichi Reader*, 2021

Because I Am So Often Alone Published in *The Ekphrastic Review*, Ekphrastic Challenge, January 2021

ANCESTRAL FABRICATIONS

Child Bride Winner, Federation of BC Writers, Literary Writes 2018 (Prose Poem); Published in *Federation of BC Writers WordWorks*, 2018

Granny Larocque, 1892, Russell, Ontario Published in *Poems from Planet Earth*, Leaf Press, 2013

Last Pinhole to the World Second Prize, The Plaza Prizes International Competition 2023 (Flash Fiction); Published in *The Plaza Prizes Anthology 1*; Shortlisted, Federation of BC Writers Literary Contest 2022 (Flash Fiction)

The Jaeger Family Theatre Shortlisted, Federation of BC Writers Literary Contest 2021 (Flash Fiction); Published in *FBCW Literary*

Sister Eugénie's Wonderful Glass Eye First Prize, Spark Anthology "Una Mujer" Literary Contest 2013 (Poetry)

Herring Radio Published in *Freefall* Vol. XXII, No. 1, 2012

What She Heard as Music Winner, The Plaza Prizes International Competition 2023 (Microfiction); Published in *The Plaza Prizes Anthology 1*; Longlisted, New Writers Flash Fiction Competition 2022

Each Cell of Your Body a Tiny Clock Longlisted, Surrey Muse Art & Literature Awards 2023 (Fiction)

A Recipe Published in *Journal of Compressed Creative Arts*, August 2013; Finalist, Writers' Union of Canada Short Fiction Contest 2011 (Microfiction)

DISORIENTATIONS

Advice While Staying in the Maasai Mara Longlisted, Bath Flash Fiction Award 2021; Published in *Bath Flash Fiction Award Anthology Six*, Snow Crow

As If the Outline of a Country Had Appeared on My Face Published in *Lesley Strutt Memorial Anthology Leap*, League of Canadian Poets 2022

FADO

Fado I Published in *CV2*, Vol. 36 No. 1, 2013

Fado II Published in *CV2*, Vol. 36 No. 1, 2013

Fado III Published in *CV2*, Vol. 36 No. 1, 2013; the author has set this text for voice and piano

Fado IV Published in *Negative Capability Press*, Winter 2020; the author has set this text for voice and piano

Fado V Published in *Voicing Suicide* anthology, Ekstasis Editions 2020

Fado VI The author has set this text for voice and piano

Fado VIII Published in *Negative Capability Press*, Winter 2020

ACKNOWLEDGEMENTS

I would like to thank my publisher Vici Johnstone, as well as Sarah Corsie, editorial & production and Malaika Aleba, marketing & publicity, at Caitlin Press for their support of this experiment in brevity and for giving life to it. I'm grateful to the British Columbia Arts Council for financial support while working on this collection, as well as the Banff Centre for Arts and Creativity for a Leighton Studio residency that allowed me to complete the manuscript.

Heartfelt thanks to flash fiction teachers and editors, including Kathy Fish, Meg Pokrass, KM Elkes, and Matt Hendrick, who shared their expertise and taught me so much about craft.

And, finally, thank you to my readers and to dear friends and family who continue to inspire me with their unwavering support, and a very special thank you to the man who makes life worth living, who never ever stops believing in me.

ABOUT THE AUTHOR

Barbara Black writes short and flash fiction, poetry and libretti. Her work has appeared in national and international publications and in many anthologies, including *Bath Flash Fiction Award 2020*. Achievements include: Fiction Finalist, *2020 National Magazine Awards*; Winner, *2017 Writers' Union of Canada Short Prose Competition*; Shortlisted, *2023 Edinburgh Flash Fiction Award*; and First and Second Prize Winner in *The Plaza Prizes Micro and Flash Fiction Contest 2023*. Her multi-award-winning debut short story collection, *Music from a Strange Planet*, was released in 2021 to critical acclaim. Black lives in Victoria, BC, where she gardens, writes and rides her trusty Triumph motorcycle.